"It won't be hard to kill the Gunsmith."

Raymond leaned back and lit a cigar, as the Sheriff shook his head in disbelief. "You don't know what you're saying. I wouldn't face the Gunsmith, even if I was backed by the three fastest guns in El Paso."

"I have no intention of sending gunfighters to kill an even better gunfighter," Raymond replied.

"Then how?"

Raymond reached down into his boot and pulled out a Bowie knife. The sinister-looking weapon sported a foot-long blade. "You're going to stick the Gunsmith?" Lola asked sharply.

"Of course not. Unless the knife-fighters I hire to kill him fail. In that case, I would consider it a great pleasure to do the job myself."

Lola nodded admiringly at Raymond. "You're as brave and smart as I always heard you were."

Don't miss any of the lusty, hard-riding action in THE GUNSMITH series

And coming from Jove
Books next month:
**THE GUNSMITH #67:
HOMESTEADER GUNS**

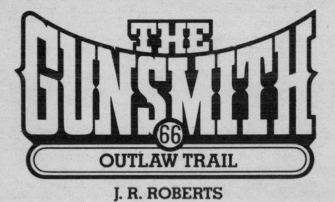

THE GUNSMITH

66

OUTLAW TRAIL

J. R. ROBERTS

CHARTER BOOKS, NEW YORK

THE GUNSMITH #66: OUTLAW TRAIL

A Charter Book / published by arrangement with
the author

PRINTING HISTORY
Charter edition / June 1987

ISBN: 0-441-30970-4

Charter Books are published by The Berkley Publishing Group,
200 Madison Avenue, New York, New York 10016.
PRINTED IN THE UNITED STATES OF AMERICA

ONE

It was a warm, humid afternoon in Ft. Worth, Texas, the kind of spring afternoon that a man like the Gunsmith preferred to enjoy indoors. So he moseyed out of his hotel room and headed for the Longhorn Saloon. The town was filled with drovers and cowboys getting ready to gather the big herds and trail them north to Wichita and Leavenworth, Kansas.

Ft. Worth was one of Clint Adams' favorite towns for the one reason that it throbbed with so much optimism and activity. There was no other place like it in the West after the Civil War, though the town itself had always attracted bold men. Back in 1849, it had been a military outpost to guard the first Texas settlers against the fierce Kiowa and Comanche Indians. Later, it became an immensely popular trading post to buffalo hunters and overland travelers. Situated in some of the world's finest cattle country, the town had soon become the recognized gathering point for the big trail herds that moved north each spring and early summer.

One of the things Clint enjoyed most was listening to the talk of the cowboys. It was fun and always humorous to hear them yarn and exaggerate about the very real dangers they would soon face on the trail. The Indians, the rivers to ford and the dry, hot country where cattle bawled with thirst and their tongues swelled up in their parched throats until they nearly choked to death.

The veteran cowboys could, if there was anyone willing to listen at all, talk for hours about stampedes, tornadoes and hailstorms so fierce they could blind a man or a beast if they were hit in the eye by one of those ice-stones. The cowboys lovingly described the trials of the job itself, the loss of sleep, contrary cattle, contrary bosses, miserable weather and the endless miles they endured in the saddle. So many miles that a man's knee and ankle joints became swollen enough that he could not yank on his pants or boots without slitting them.

Clint enjoyed these kinds of stories. He was one of the few men who recognized that this was a very special moment in American history that would never be repeated. In five, ten years at the most, the range would be fenced off and the great northern cattle trails would be no more as nesters and sod-busters chopped up the land into little bits and pieces. But Clint had learned not to tell that to the young cowboys he listened to. They believed that they and trail drives would live forever. The Gunsmith understood that very well; when he had been their age, he had thought that a good lawman never died. All that was required was that he be the fastest man on earth with a six-gun. There were many men, both dead and planted on Boot Hill, who could attest to Clint's remarkable ability with a Colt, but he knew that being fast and being accurate were not enough. Over the years, you also had to be damned lucky that some drunken fool did not draw his gun and shoot you in the back, or that some vengeful bastard did not ambush you from a rooftop or alley. Clint Adams stayed in the law business as long as he figured his luck could hold and when he believed he had pushed it beyond the normal limit, he prudently took up the trade of gunsmithing.

He had never regretted the decision, but neither did he waste time thinking about all the outlaws and would-be gunfighters he had faced and shot dead. And why should he? After all, he had never killed anyone who hadn't tried to kill him first.

"Howdy, Gunsmith!" swaggering, bowlegged cowboys called as he passed down the boardwalk.

Clint acknowledged every greeting. He was a well-known and highly respected man, even among the cowboys who were still too young to shave. The Gunsmith might be ten or fifteen years their senior, but he moved with the grace of a man who had never abused his body on one of those grueling cattle drives or been busted up by a horse, or trampled by a fractious longhorn steer. He was also a natural athlete with extraordinary reflexes and balance. His hand and eye coordination was so exceptional that he could draw and point his gun before most men even started their play. But then, if you were a gunfighter, there was no room for mediocrity.

"Why the hell don't you join our boys and drive some cattle up the long trail," a cattleman by the name of Ed Stamp said as he clapped the Gunsmith on the shoulder and they pushed through the bat-wing doors into the Longhorn Saloon. "Clint, you keep coming here every spring and listening to all the stories, you ought to join us and find out what it's really like."

"No thanks," Clint replied as he edged up to the bar and ordered a beer for himself and one for the cattle rancher. "If it's half—even a quarter—as miserable as it seems, then I want no part of it. Besides, my horse, Duke, he doesn't know a cow from an antelope and that's the way I like him."

"You been racing him any this year?"

Clint shook his head. The truth was, his big black gelding was so well known for his speed in this part of Texas that he could not get any bettors.

"I heard of a red Kentucky stallion in town that is supposed to be faster 'n the tongue of a bullfrog. The man who owns him is giving two-to-one odds against anyone who will race his horse."

Clint's ears perked up. "That a fact?"

"Sure is."

"You think he would race Duke?"

Ed shrugged. "He might. I seen the horse. It's a Kentucky thoroughbred and is every bit as tall as Duke. Thing of it is, the man won't race anyone for less than two miles."

"Two miles!" The Gunsmith paid for the beers and handed one to the rancher. "That's absurd in this heat and humidity."

"I know. I know. The man has a little jockey about four feet tall that looks like he would kill you for a quarter. I got a feeling that the pair would be impossible to beat."

"Two miles is way too damn far. I'm not interested in running Duke like that."

"I agree, but I thought I'd pass the word along. Seems pretty likely this fella will hear about you and Duke anyway and come seeking you out."

"Let him," Clint said. "I'm not interested."

"Sure," the rancher said. "Only I can't believe the Gunsmith I know would ever refuse a challenge."

Clint smiled. "The odds are fine. If the man will drop the distance to one mile, I think we can have ourselves a horse race. I'm a little low on cash and that horse and I are used to eating everyday."

The rancher laughed. "Clint, I will pay you thirty a month and found if you join my crew."

"No thank you. Maybe next year."

The rancher laughed even louder as he downed his beer and moved over to talk to some of the others drovers. It had been a standing joke between Clint and Ed Stamp for three years running and the man got a bigger hoot out of it with each passing spring.

Clint turned to watch a strikingly handsome young blonde he had seen a few times before working as a shill to the crowd. He did not know her name, but he had been attracted to her almost immediately. Now, she was standing beside the piano player and had started singing "The Old Chisholm Trail." But the piano was out of tune and its player was either drunk or hungover so badly he could not find the right keys. He kept hitting the wrong notes and even though the girl was doing her best to cover up for him, she was creating a lot of laughter and some pretty unkind ridicule.

Clint did not like that. He frowned and sipped his beer. In honesty, the girl had a lousy singing voice. She missed the high notes and overshot the low ones. But she was so petite and innocent looking that she reminded him of an angel. Her long, blonde hair was brushed to a shine and she had the bluest eyes he had ever seen on any woman. But right now, those eyes were clouded with a mixture of anger and concern as the crowd poked fun at her and the player.

She should have quit, but Clint saw a stubbornness to the fine set of her jaw. She had started the damn song and she was going to finish it come hell or high water. And she would have, too, if a big cowboy had not started catawalling like a timber wolf.

Tears welled up in the girl's eyes and she stopped in the middle of her song. With everyone watching, she strode up to the cowboy and slapped his face so hard he staggered off balance.

The music died. The cowboy flushed with humiliation and then he did something that caused the Gunsmith to slam his beer down hard.

The big cowboy slapped the pretty blonde singer back. The crack of his huge fist was like a shot of lightning across a prairie sky. The girl cried out and went reeling into the piano. Men who, moments before, had been making fun of the singer and piano player were no longer smiling.

There was an unspoken law out West that men did not lay hands on women, at least those they weren't married to or that weren't whores. And even in those two cases it was considered a sign of viciousness and unmanliness to beat or strike a woman.

"She's nothing but a high-priced whore!" the huge cowboy yelled, aware that the crowd had suddenly united with anger and disapproval. "She had no right to slap me first and I'll be goddamn if any whore can do that to Jack Wheeler and get away with it!"

The blonde shook her head and started to come at Wheeler with curved fingernails but Clint saw the cowboy ball up his fist to hit her. He knew that the next blow would bust up the girl's lovely face.

"Hold it!" he shouted.

Wheeler spun around and his hand streaked for his gun. But Clint had anticipated that and his own Colt seemed to leap into his fist.

Wheeler froze before his gun left his holster. His eyes bulged and then, he slowly sagged with defeat as his hand released his gun butt. "I can't beat a goddamn professional gunfighter," he hissed. "If you kill me, you'll hang to murder. Everybody see this. My gun is in its holster and I am not going to draw on the Gunsmith!"

Clint's lip curled with contempt. "And I suppose

you think this means that you can get away with slapping that young lady and..."

Wheeler brayed like a mule. He was well over six feet tall and built like an ox. He had coarse features and deep-set black eyes that were as unfeeling as pieces of coal. The man was obviously used to having his way. "I told you she ain't no lady! I screwed her last night and she took twenty dollars for it. Hell, I..."

Clint saw pain spring into the eyes of the girl and heard her gasp with humiliation. She seemed to shrink before the crowd as Wheeler's cruel words slashed like knives.

The Gunsmith had seen and heard enough. He couldn't shoot this man like he deserved, but he damn sure wasn't going to allow him to tear a woman apart in front of a crowd.

It just was not right.

Clint doubled up his fists giving several inches and a lot of pounds of muscle to the man he faced. With a growl in his throat, he moved forward determined to close the big man's mouth.

Wheeler saw him coming, realized what the Gunsmith was going to do and smiled with anticipation. Now, he seemed to think, with bare knuckles instead of bullets, the advantage is all mine!

He could not have been more mistaken.

TWO

When a man with a reputation for having a fast gun allowed himself to be goaded into a common fistfight, he was either desperate or stupid. Fistfighters busted up their hands and knuckles; gunfighters were very careful to protect their fingers and hands. Clint was neither stupid nor desperate, but he was mad plain through and through.

He figured he had the advantage in experience and speed yet knew that the bigger, stronger, younger man he faced could win in a toe-to-toe slugfest. That's why Clint ducked Jack Wheeler's roundhouse swing instead of trying to block it and getting knocked backwards by the force. He ducked and then his own fist whistled upward to bury itself deep in Wheeler's gut and shaped the huge man like a bent nail. When Wheeler's mouth flew open like a landed fish sucking for water, Clint stepped back and pounded a solid overhand left to the cowboy's cheek that opened it to the bone and sent the more powerful cowboy back-pedaling to the wall.

The crowd hooted and clapped their hands with

8

lusty approval. It was obvious that the Gunsmith was the smaller man, for once the underdog. By all rights, he had foolishly forfeited his advantage and should have been whipped pretty fast by the powerful young cowboy. But now, as Clint advanced with his hands moving fast enough to blur, the crowd was cheering.

Wheeler was tough and game. After Clint banged him three or four wicked blows to the face, Wheeler grabbed the Gunsmith and hurled him spinning across the room. Clint struck a faro table and the players all went crashing over spilling cards and chips. Before Clint could recover, Jack Wheeler kicked him in the ribs and sent him sprawling on the floor.

"Get up and fight!" Wheeler shouted exultantly.

Clint winced as he gathered his feet underneath his body. Wheeler's kick had cracked a couple of his lower ribs and that was a painful way to go at a man. But he stood up and they circled each other warily. Clint was about six feet tall but slender enough that he looked much smaller than the man he faced.

"Gunsmith, you shore should have stayed out of this," Wheeler said with a shake of his massive head. "I—"

Clint's left darted out and his stiff jab snapped Wheeler's head back and knocked him off balance. Clint followed it with a right cross that had all of his strength behind it and the bigger man's nose sprouted blood.

"You broke it!" Wheeler shouted, wiping his bloodied nose with the back of his sleeve. "I'm gonna break your neck for that."

"Come and get it," Clint said, his hands up and ready.

Wheeler charged like an infuriated bull. His momentum carried him forward but Clint ducked again and slammed two more shots into the man's ribs. His fists bounced off Wheeler and the man grunted. But hitting the massive cowboy was like punching a side of beef.

Wheeler turned around, his face smeared crimson and his lips pulled back in a snarl. He didn't lunge at the Gunsmith anymore, but instead came wading in with short, brutal punches. Clint took one on the point of his chin. He dropped and Wheeler tried to stomp his head in.

The girl screamed and jumped on Wheeler's back. She clawed his face and pulled him off balance. He roared and slung her away, but by then Clint was on his feet and his fist was streaking back to the broken nose of his opponent.

He connected and the force of his blow was so great it sent a wave of pain the entire length of his arm. Jack Wheeler bellowed in pain and cupped his face in both hands. Clint drove two booming uppercuts to the man's solar plexus and Wheeler sagged. The cowboy's tree-trunk sized legs seemed to go rubbery and Clint chopped him to the sawdust covered floor with a mighty sledging blow that landed just behind the ear.

Wheeler hit the floor and bounced. He was out cold. The crowd seemed to expel a deep breath and then everyone was grabbing Clint and hauling him to the bar.

The Gunsmith needed something stronger than beer right now. He gratefully accepted a couple of shots of whiskey that were shoved into each of his two swelling fists. He poured one down and started to pour another when someone shouted, "Wheeler has his gun out!"

Clint threw both arms out and knocked men aside as he stood alone to face Jack Wheeler. Wheeler who knelt and was trying to stand but whose six-gun looked like a cannon. Clint's own swollen fist strayed toward his side arm.

Wheeler cocked his weapon and hissed, "Go ahead, make it self-defense for me, Gunsmith."

Clint pulled his hand away. He was fast, but not faster than it took a man to simply pull his trigger. And at a distance of less than twenty feet, Jack Wheeler would not miss.

"Beg for your life or so help me you are a dead man," Wheeler said in a twisted, hate-ravaged voice. "Get down on your knees and beg me for your life!"

Clint blinked. He took a deep breath and let it out slowly. He simply could not do it, not even to save his life. "No."

"Fine. You die then!"

A gun boomed and a cloud of blue smoke mushroomed out from the .44 derringer in the blonde's fist. Jack Wheeler took the bullet through his heart and he stood up on his toes as if beginning a minuet of death. Then his feet tangled up and he crashed like an oak tree. Clint knew the man was dead before he struck the floor.

The girl's eyes filled with tears and she sniffled as she stuffed the derringer in a secret place in her dress. There wasn't a sound in the room until the piano player tapped a chord and said, "Rosalie, why don't we just finish our song?"

The girl blinked and then she nodded and began to sing. Her voice was high and quavery, but she finished the song giving it all she had and men in the Longhorn Saloon understood what kind of courage that took. When she was finished, the crowd began to cheer and everyone stepped over the dead man and rushed to the bar to order drinks. Not surprisingly, Clint and Rosalie were the center of attention and found themselves being plied with free drinks.

It was sometime later that they were able to extract themselves from the crowd of admirers and move over to a table where they could talk.

Rosalie raised a glass to Clint and said, "You, sir, are my brave and handsome gentleman."

Clint touched his swollen cheek and tried to ignore the throbbing ache of his cracked ribs. "Not so handsome, especially not after that."

They both watched the owner of the bar and another employee drag the dead Jack Wheeler into the back room and slam the door shut. A few minutes later, the owner stomped by and it was clear that he was furious.

"You're fired, Rosalie! I can't have my help shooting my damned customers!"

"But—"

"Fired!" he shouted as he stormed out the door, probably headed for the undertaker's office.

Rosalie downed her drink and sniffled into a lace handkerchief. "Well," she said fatalistically, "I guess there goes my singing career and my job all at the same time."

Clint reached across the table and patted her bare arm. He was aware of her perfume and her beauty was almost as intoxicating as the whiskey. "You can always find another job. There are at least a dozen saloons in Ft. Worth."

"Sure, but you heard me sing. Admit it. I'm awful!"

This admission caught Clint unawares. "Well," he hedged. "I can't say as how you have the best voice I ever heard, but not the worst either."

Her eyes misted. "I'll never make it as a singer. I can't sing and I can't dance. I can't play the piano or anything but . . ."

She reached for the bottle of whiskey someone had

bought for them and she poured herself a full glass. "I guess I know what a girl like me, given what everyone in this saloon heard from Jack Wheeler, has coming. I have no choice now. I might as well put a mattress on my back and move into the alley and set up shop."

"Stop it!" Clint said angrily. "You're not a whore!"

She broke down and cried. It took almost five wretched minutes to get her calmed down and Clint hated every one of them. Crying women tore him apart. "Here," he said, "let's go find a quiet place to talk. You need some fresh air and sunshine."

He led her through the door and, for a minute, her spirits seemed to lift but then someone joked loud enough for all to hear, "Look at the Gunsmith! Bet he don't have to pay for it like Jack did last night!"

The saloon resounded with ribald laughter and by the time Clint got Rosalie out to the street, she was reduced to tears again.

"Never mind them," he said. "They don't know what the hell they are talking about."

"Yes they do, Clint," she said as he helped her to a shady bench underneath a tree. "Because the truth is, Jack Wheeler told the truth when he said I took money from him for using me."

"Oh." Clint frowned. He did not know what else to say.

She reached out and took his hand. "Clint, I guess this makes you feel pretty foolish, having stood up for a woman's virtue only to discover that she has no virtue. But if it makes you feel any better at all, I can honestly say that I never took money for making love before. Not ever. And . . . and I hope I never will again, but . . ."

"Aw," he said, watching her eyes tear up and her

shoulders start to shake up and down, "don't go cry-ing on me again, Rosalie! I can't stand to see a pretty girl cry."

"I'm not pretty anymore! My face is swollen up worse than yours! And I lost my job and I have no place to go and can't do anything anyway and—"

"Whoa up!" he cried before she really started raining. "Things can't be that bad. Not for a girl as young and pretty as you are. And . . . and I'll help you find something."

She looked up. Faint hope burned through the tears. "You will?"

"I'll try."

She squealed happily and threw her arms around him and squeezed. Clint cried out in pain. "Ribs! My ribs are cracked!"

"I'm sorry!" she cried. "Oh, dear. And it's all my fault. Come with me. I'll bandage them for you. My father, he was a doctor and showed me how to do all kinds of things. Set bones, bandage wounds, stuff like that."

"You said 'was a doctor.' Why did he quit?"

"One of his patients died during surgery and the man's wife shot and killed my father. It was awful."

Clint swallowed. "Yeah, that is awful," he agreed as he let her gently usher him to the Baltimore Hotel where he was staying. After all, she had nowhere to go and her father had been a doctor.

THREE

"What a nice room you have!" she said as she helped him inside to the bed. She grabbed a pillow, fluffed it up expertly and eased it under his head. "Just stretch out and I'll go find some bandages to wrap those poor old ribs of yours."

Clint nodded and closed his eyes. He had taken some fearfully hard punches from Jack Wheeler. One pile-driving right in particular had nearly taken off the side of his face. Now that the whiskey and the excitement were wearing off, Clint began to feel all the battle wounds he had just sustained.

He pitched the girl his room key. "Bring back something to eat and drink. Also some medicinal powder and liniment for a shoulder muscle I seem to have pulled during the fight."

"You were so wonderful! And to think you did it for me!"

She blew him a happy kiss and left after locking the door. It was true; he had fought for her, but also, he would have done the same thing for any woman. It was a matter of honor and being able to live with yourself. It was the Gunsmith's code and, this time, it conveniently worked for a woman that he found very, very desirable.

Clint gingerly examined his ribs. Maybe they weren't broken at all; maybe just bruised. He sure hoped so and would probably know for sure in the morning. But it would not hurt to have them bandaged tightly.

He undressed and eased into bed. In only a moment, he was asleep.

She woke him as the sun was setting and the day cooling off nicely. A soft summer rain pattered on the rooftop and the smell of wood and wet dust drifted thickly up from the streets of Ft. Worth. He also smelled Rosalie and her perfume was heady in his nostrils.

She was in bed with him and the touch of her smooth, cool skin was like a balm. "I need you to sit up, darling, while I wrap this bandage around those poor ribs a few times," she whispered.

He groaned but obeyed. She tossed the covers off them and sat up with the bandage and a pair of scissors. He opened his eyes wide with appreciation. Rosalie was prettier than one of those nude pictures you saw over the back bar. And a lot more slender. In the fading light, her skin was as smooth and white as spun silk. She had a narrow waist and girlish hips but her breasts were as full as those of a big woman, firm and lifting proudly.

Clint reached out and his fingers brushed her thigh. She shivered and teased, "you're an injured man, Clint. A man with broken ribs and many bruises. What you need is rest."

He did not agree and neither did his stiffening manhood. "What I need is something to make me forget the pain. Something like you, Rosalie."

"But . . . well, all right. To try to protest would be entirely contrary to my own desires."

He smiled. Pulled her down close until her breasts hung like ripe and golden fruit from a tree. He closed his mouth over one of them and smacked his lips. "Nice, Rosalie, very nice."

She giggled and wiggled. "Try the other, sir."

He did and it was every bit as good. Clint nibbled and sucked gently until he felt her hands moving over his body with some urgency. He reached for her and she spread herself wide as he rolled onto her.

"Are you sure about those . . . ohh, that feels so good," she moaned. "About those . . ."

"Ribs," he reminded her, as she grabbed his big staff and guided it into her warm wetness.

She swallowed noisily. Made a small, pleasurable sound deep in her throat. "Yes, you're . . . so wonderfully big!"

He laughed but stopped instantly because it hurt his ribs. Maybe, he thought as he began to move inside of her, working his hips around and around in full, deep circles, they really are cracked.

But later, when she lost control and wrapped her legs around him and began to buck and cry out with ecstasy, he decided that his ribs could not possibly be hurt very much.

That decided, Clint let his body move at its own surging, quickening pace. He stirred her through one grasping, clutching climax after another until he lost track of space and time. He grunted and then his hard body spasmed and spewed his seed deep into her slick, perfect little body.

Afterward, she wrapped his ribs but it seemed almost pointless and had it not given her such obvious pleasure, Clint would have dispensed with it entirely.

"Will you really help me find an exciting but honest job?" she asked him later that night as they lay close together.

"Exciting? You never said anything about excitement being a part of it."

Rosalie moved away from him a little and said, "But I thought you could see that I was not the kind of girl who could do something ordinary like waiting on tables in some greasy cafe or on fat, fussy old women in a millinery store."

Clint scowled in the night. "What, exactly, did you have in mind?"

"I don't know. But I've always worked in saloons and exciting places."

"I bet they were exciting. You were probably real busy trying to keep cowboys from dragging you under the tables."

She giggled. "Once, I worked for a drummer who sold snake oil and medicine out of the back of his wagon. He was nice to me and treated me like his daughter. No funny business except when he drank too much of his own medicine and got drunk. But then, I could lock him either in or out of his wagon and sleep alone. It was fun. Almost as much fun as when I raced horses and—"

Clint blinked in the darkness. "You raced horses?"

"As a girl I did. My father owned a bunch of them and I was his jockey. I rode them until I was sixteen and then I had a bad spill. After that, my father made me quit."

"What about your mother?"

"I never knew her," Rosalie said. "She died giving birth to me."

"I'm sorry."

"So am I."

"Rosalie?"

"Yes?"

"How would you like to earn some real good money riding my horse in a race?"

She sat up fast. "Do you mean it?"

"Sure!"

"Can your horse run?"

"Can ducks walk on water?" It was a ridiculous question designed to make her laugh. Clint thought she had a wonderful laugh, surprisingly low and throaty for a woman who barely topped five feet.

"I don't know and I don't care. But do you have a really fast horse?"

"As fast as you ever rode," he said. "Would you like to see him?"

"Tonight?"

"Sure," Clint said, rolling out of bed and grabbing his shirt and pants. "He's down at the stable. Come on, get dressed. The way you're put together, you'd cause a damn riot if you went out without your clothes."

Rosalie bubbled with her laughter. "Clint," she said, "you and I are going to have some fun and maybe even make some good money!"

"If you can really ride, we will."

"Ha!" she cried. "I can ride, the question is, can your horse run!"

"You'll find out soon enough," Clint promised, as he helped her pull on her blouse and they headed for the livery.

FOUR

•

Two days later, the man that owned the red Kentucky stallion found Clint and Rosalie having lunch on the veranda of the Del Rio Hotel.

"Excuse me for the interruption, but aren't you the famous Gunsmith?"

Clint looked up to see a short, heavy-set man with a bald head and a gold tooth beaming at him. The man was dressed expensively, new bowler in his hand, silk tie, starched white shirt and polished black shoes. But even with the well-cut suit, he somehow managed to look seedy and disreputable. And just behind him stood what reminded Clint of a gargoyle, one of those grotesque little creatures that raised the hair on the back of your neck. The man was very short, even shorter than Rosalie and while his legs were bowed and slender, his upper torso was broad and rippled with muscle. He had tiny hands and feet but his forearms were as thick and corded as the twisted roots of trees. Clint knew at once that this was the jockey.

"My name, sir, is Samuel Lockerel and this is my assistant, Bennie."

The little man grinned, first at Clint, but then at Rosalie as his hot little eyes surveyed her ample busom. Clint saw the young woman actually shiver with revulsion. He decided right then that he would not allow Rosalie to ride Duke against this professional jockey.

"What can I do for you?"

"I would have thought you'd heard the talk by now," Lockerel said expansively. "Apparently, it is an established fact that you and I have the two fastest horses in this entire city. Perhaps even in all of Texas."

"Possibly, but I'm not interested in a race."

"Oh come now!" Lockerel cried. "The whole town is abuzz over the prospect. Bets are already being placed in every saloon and, down in the stockyards, there is nothing but talk of your horse and mine racing to capture the pride of Ft. Worth."

Rosalie grabbed his arm. "Clint, you promised I could ride Duke! What's wrong?"

He sighed. He had promised but . . . but dammit! Couldn't she see the kind of twisted creature she'd be riding against? "Why don't we discuss this alone?"

"What's to discuss!" Lockerel cried. "You have a magnificent racing horse, and so do I. Isn't that the real issue? They were born to run, man! I say let's see which is the fastest."

"Duke isn't a racehorse," Clint said stiffly. "He just happens to be very, very fast. I use him everyday. He is a working animal."

Lockerel chuckled almost obscenely. "Oh, be reasonable. Don't try and tell me that your animal is a common cowpony! Bennie and I have already taken the liberty of visiting his stall. The creature is magnificent! Almost the equal of my stallion, Crimson Victory. I call the horse "Vic" for short, but the former is his registered name. What is the pedigree of your animal, sir?"

"Beats the hell out of me," Clint said peevishly. "His name is Duke. Period."

Lockerel shrugged. "What does a pedigree and a fancy name matter anyway? Even mongrel beasts have been known to be able to run."

Clint half rose from his chair. "Mongrel beasts!"

Lockerel stepped back quickly. "Sir, I hope you understand that I mean no insult. A good, common horse is not to be made fun of even if they do look plow-horsey."

Clint slammed his fist down so hard that their goblets of water splashed all over the linen. "That ties it! How much money are we talking?"

Lockerel's golden tooth vanished. Now that he had his man in the game, there was no need to be ingratiating. "How much do you have?"

"Enough." That wasn't entirely true. Clint was down to less than three hundred dollars in cash, but his name was good for five times that much.

"Five hundred too rich for your blood, Gunsmith? I know that you are semi-retired and probably don't earn a great deal fixing old weapons for a little pocket money, but—"

"Five hundred dollars it is! But I will not run my animal more than one mile."

"One mile? Pshaah!" Lockerel exclaimed, puckering his lips as if he had bitten into a sour lemon. "Crimson Victory is a thoroughbred, sir! Not some squatty, bandy-legged mustang good for a couple of hundred yards and then nothing. Two miles is an honorable distance."

"It's a killing distance in this heat and humidity. I won't do it."

Bennie the jockey sneered. "Which one of you

isn't up to the task, sir. You or the black gelding?"

"Neither." Clint eyed them coldly. "One mile."

Lockerel shrugged. "I guess I will have to inform the good men of Ft. Worth that the esteemed Gunsmith and his over-regarded gelding refused to race."

Clint had been baited enough. "You tell them whatever you want, mister. I've raced Duke a dozen times in Texas and he has never lost. You're the one who has something to prove with your animal, not me."

"Very well then!" Lockerel stormed. "A mile and one half, sir. That is the minimum I will race for anything less is a travesty. Will you accept?"

"Clint," Rosalie pleaded, "I can ride Duke and beat them!"

"She's ridin' the black," Bennie said, his eyes widening just a little. He rubbed his powerful jockey's hands over his overlarge jaw. "Tough game for a sweet young woman to be in."

"I am tough!"

"No offense, ma'am, I just thought that since the horse belongs to the Gunsmith, he oughta be the man in the saddle."

"Why should I be?" Clint demanded. "You don't own bloody old Vic, do you?"

Bennie colored and looked away. He reached for a plug of tobacco and ripped it in two, then shoved a big wad into his mouth and chewed furiously.

"A race it is," Clint said. "Rosalie . . ."

"Rosie," she corrected. "That's what most people call me anyhow and Rosalie just sounds too sweet for a jockey. Don't you think?"

"Sure, Rosie." Clint turned his attention back to Lockerel. "When shall we race?"

"Tomorrow is Saturday. Sunday is the best day of the week. I say Sunday at one o'clock. Does that suit you?"

"Yeah. We'll race out of town, circle a wagon three-quarters of a mile out, then come on back."

"No," Lockerel said. "A thoroughbred is not born to turn quickly once it is in full stride. I propose we simply take a turn about the town and leave it at that."

Clint wasn't too sure. If Rosie raced straight out and straight back, Clint could keep a better eye on her and watch for any of Bennie's skulduggery.

"Please, Clint. I'll be all right. He'll be eating my dust every foot of the way."

Clint nodded but with serious misgivings. Duke was the kind of horse that would kill himself to win, but he was not adverse to keeping it a close race. In fact, he seemed to enjoy racing neck and neck with an opponent and then surging ahead at the tape.

"It's your race," he said. "But it's my horse. All right. Once around town and then it is done."

"Excellent!" Lockerel cried. "And who shall hold the purses?"

"The bank of Ft. Worth. Fella there named William Tippett. He'll take your deposit." Clint knew he would also have to borrow some money to deposit with the banker.

"Fine," Lockerel said, rubbing his hands together rapidly. "Sunday, one o'clock. That will give us time to make sure we have a roaring big crowd on hand."

Bennie shouldered between them, bowed his ugly little head and then grinned at Rosie. "May the best rider and horse win," he said. "And I wish you a safe journey."

Clint clamped his hand down on the man's powerful shoulder. "You hurt this girl and you'll answer to me!"

Bennie shrugged away and his face was malicious. "Don't threaten me, Gunsmith! I been winning races since you was in knee pants. This is to be a horse race, not a goddamn tea social. Horses bump into each other and they have even been known to fall and break their necks. If you want a woman to ride your animal, she has to be ready for anything."

"I'll put a bullet through your brainpan if you slash her or my horse with a whip," Clint said, in a deadly voice. "I want that understood right here and now."

Bennie grinned and said, "I'll do whatever I have to do to win the race. She had better be ready to do the same."

"You've been warned. Both of you."

Lockerel's eyes went cold. "Threats are unnecessary and unworthy of men with our sterling reputations. Come Bennie, we must get our horse ready for Sunday."

They watched them stalk away. Clint was no longer hungry. He had completely lost his appetite.

Rosie patted him on the arm. "Don't look so worried. Duke and I can beat them."

"In a fair race, I think you probably could, but I can't shake the feeling that it will be fair only as long as they are certain of winning. Rosie, from now until Sunday, we must sleep, live and eat in the stall next to Duke. I would not put it past them to doctor the horse in order to win by forfeit."

"Good idea. And maybe I ought to ride Duke a time or two before the race."

"Yes," Clint said, already wishing he had not allowed himself to be goaded into this contest. "I think that would be an excellent idea."

FIVE

Sunday dawned hot and humid but no one seemed to care as men gathered in the streets and in small knots out at the edges of town. All the talk was of the race. Several herds had even delayed their departure for Kansas because their crews threatened to walk away if they could not see and bet on this historic run. Since news of the contest had been announced, there had been a steady stream of visitors to the livery and yesterday, when Clint and Rosie had gone out to exercise Duke, big crowds followed.

"I have never seen such excitement as this!" Rosie exclaimed as she returned from a light Sunday morning workout on Duke. "Look at all the people. This is really exciting."

"How did it feel?" Clint asked as he helped Rosie down from his big gelding.

"He felt wonderful." Rosie's eyes sparkled. "I've never ridden anything like your horse. He is so smooth and powerful." She reached out and touched him intimately. "Like his master," she said.

26

Clint blushed because there was a crowd around them. They were cowboys and ranchers, townspeople and merchants, gamblers, bronc busters and even prostitutes. The word was that the red stallion was not as impressive as first thought.

But Clint knew better than that. Lockerel and Bennie would purposefully make their animal appear uneven of stride and overly nervous. They would want the best odds they could get and they did that by making Duke appear to be the clearly superior animal.

"You can't lose," a cowboy said loud enough for the dozens around him to hear. "This here is a real horse, that other'n is all legs and he has no balance. This animal ever work cattle?"

"Nope," the Gunsmith replied as he removed the light racing saddle he had borrowed and started to rub Duke down with a gunnysack.

"He should win anyway," the cowboy said with an emphatic nod of his head. "Jest let him get flat out and it's a sure thing."

"Thanks for the great advice," Clint said shortly. In truth, it was lousy advice. The temperature was in the mid-nineties and, with the humidity, it seemed like over a hundred degrees. Even though both horses were in top physical condition, they would have to be paced so that they had a closing finish.

The morning wore on slowly. Clint tried to keep Duke in the livery, but the crowds became so big he had to spirit the horse out the back way and they hid in a small abandoned barn for a few quiet hours.

"Clint?"

He looked to the girl. Was she finally getting nervous? Thus far, she had acted as if she were a young girl going on a Sunday picnic. And whenever he had tried to tell her that Bennie might try and slash her with his whip or even knock her flying, she had abruptly changed the subject as if such a thing were impossible.

"If Duke wins, what would you do?"

"What do you mean? I'd collect the money and be five hundred richer."

"But . . . but would you want to go into pardners? I mean, travel around and race this horse? We could go out to California where no one knows him and make a fortune."

"Not interested in that kind of a life," Clint said. "I'll not back down from a challenge and I like a good race as well as the next man but I don't want to make it a business."

"Why not? Isn't Duke really fast enough?"

"I don't know," Clint said. "I think he is, but there are probably faster horses somewhere. He's no colt anymore and hard racing will break down the best horse's legs. It's just not something I want to do, Rosie."

"But what am I supposed to do after this race? I have to have something. You've got a trade. What have I got? Nothing."

Clint frowned. "I told you I'd ask about for a job. I just haven't had time, what with all this commotion going on. But I will."

"No you won't," she said quietly. "You won't because there is nothing I can do except some drudgery or becoming a—"

"Don't even say it," Clint warned. "Just put that kind of thinking out of your pretty head."

"Would you ever want to get married?" Rosie asked, moving to close to press herself up tight against him. "We could make a great team."

He kissed her. Felt the heat rise in his loins. This woman had a powerful effect on him that way. A powerful effect! But he had to be honest. "No,

Rosie, I am not the marrying kind."

She sighed and kissed him on the cheek. "I knew that before I asked. I just don't see much of a future between us, darling."

Clint shrugged. "We can enjoy each other awhile and then I'll move on. But I'll see to it that you are doing something you like and that will support you decently."

"Thank you," she said, but there was no warmth in her words.

Clint stood near the two horses. The crowd was dead silent and the race was about to begin. Crimson Victory was a beautiful animal, about the same height as Duke but much finer boned and high strung. The thoroughbred danced and the crowd stared in admiration. Bennie was dressed in purple racing tights. Up on the back of the big stallion, he looked almost natural.

Rosie swallowed nervously. Clint patted her knee. "Just let the horse run but hold him in a little bit. Stay close but not so close that Bennie can whip you."

"All right."

"Are you ready," the race official asked.

The two riders nodded. The man looked to the starter who raised his gun. Suddenly, it exploded and the two horses lunged forward, then shot out of town. It had been decided that they would finish the race exactly where they had begun it. Clint headed for the rooftop of the Del Rio. It was the tallest building in town and would give him a view of almost half the race. But it was the other half that he was really worried about. The part where the racecourse dipped behind some low hills for about three hundred yards.

That was where Rosie would be on her own.

SIX

Rosie let the Duke run and his great power seemed to flow into her as she raced neck and neck beside the red stallion. Bennie kept glancing sideways at her but his face was a mask. He rode as if he were a part of the horse, and Rosie tried to emulate his style until she realized that the race would be over before she could even begin to figure out how he appeared to hang over the stallion's withers so that his weight was perfectly balanced.

Duke edged ahead but it was clear that the two animals were just pacing themselves for the second half of the race. Then, suddenly, Bennie smacked his whip across the rump of the thoroughbred and the big animal flattened its ears and seemed to bound forward with wings on its feet. One minute Rosie figured she had the race perfectly in hand, and the very next she was falling behind.

"Come on, Duke, we can't let him run away from us!"

The black gelding had no intention of letting anyone run away from him. Duke seemed to settle down

lower to the ground and his body began to stretch
and pull with a power that rocked her back in her
saddle. The big gelding shot forward and, to Rosie's
joy, actually closed the distance until they were running neck and neck.

They swung into the low hills where the town disappeared from sight. Duke edged up to match the
stallion stride for stride and then he actually began to
inch ahead. Bennie grinned and then used his whip
across her back. Rosie cried out in pain and urged
Duke faster, but Bennie caught her twice more across
the arms so that she almost dropped the reins. She bit
back tears and swung Duke wide, but the jockey anticipated that and slashed his stallion until it closed in.
Bennie tried to kick her out of the saddle.

"Damn you!" Rosie cried as she fought him. "Get
away!"

Bennie hissed and this time his whip stung her
across the ear. Rosie almost fell. Her eyes filled with
tears and she cried, "I'll get you for this!"

She saw Bennie raise his whip to strike her again
and she ducked. The blow whistled overhead and
Bennie lost his balance enough to throw the stallion
off-stride for just a moment. It was enough to send
Duke into the lead.

Bennie shouted, "Seven hundred dollars to you if
you pull him in, Rosie! Seven hundred dollars!"

"Ha!" she yelled, "I'd never see a penny of it!"

"I'll give it to you right now!"

Rosie needed that money worse than she had ever
needed anything. Seven hundred dollars would give
her enough to pay Clint for his loss and net her a
clear two hundred dollar profit. With that kind of
money, she could finally have a start at something.
She had never had a break in her entire life, never
had more than a hundred dollars all at once. And
Clint would leave her before long.

"Seven hundred and you pull the black in now!" Bennie shouted as he dug into his racing tunic and yanked out a sheaf of fifty dollar bills. "Everybody but the suckers win!"

Rosie understood what the jockey was saying. They had the betting money and the odds to win heavy. Now, Rosie looked back and saw the money and damn her if she did not feel her arms begin to pull Duke up a stride until she and the jockey were riding side by side, slowing their horses.

"Give it to me!" she cried, reaching for it, sure that he would grab her hand and pull her to the earth. But if he did, she would tell the race officials and the Gunsmith. Clint would insist on another race and he'd probably get it . . . and even if that failed, Bennie and his master would face the Gunsmith's wrath. "If this is a trick, you know what he'll do to you."

"We know. Take the goddamn money. We're coming out of the hills!"

Rosie took the money. Guilt crushed her. She felt like dirt, but then she'd felt even worse when she remembered what she had let Jack Wheeler do to her for a lousy twenty dollars. She pulled Duke into a choppy gallop as the stallion swept past. She counted the money and it was all there. Seven hundred dollars. Clint would be furious, but he'd understand and they would all win. Dammit, they really would!

Duke was surging against the rein, fighting the bit. And then they were shooting out of the hills and the stallion was six lengths ahead. Rosie stuffed the money into her blouse and fought the big gelding until her arms ached and there was less than a quarter mile to go.

But then, she heard the crowd and saw the huge throngs of men and women. And she heard them all shouting and pleading for her and Duke to overtake the fancy thoroughbred stallion. She saw cowboys angling in on their own ponies, waving their Stetsons and shouting themselves hoarse because they had bet everything on the black horse they knew should honestly win.

"Aw dammit!" Rosie cried, "I can't do this!"

She gave Duke his head and the gelding faltered, suddenly caught by surprise. "Go on and run!" Rosie shouted, drumming her heels into Duke's ribs.

Bennie heard her shouts growing louder as Duke surged at the stallion. The veteran jockey turned in his saddle and saw the gelding devouring the prairie in monstrous bounds. He whipped at the stallion furiously and then hunched down low on the animal's withers and prepared to give Crimson Victory the ride of his life.

The black gelding ran like a thing possessed. His powerful legs clawed for distance and the breath tore in and out of his massive chest. They closed and then ran dead even for twenty strides as Crimson Victory gave it everything he possessed.

Bennie cursed as his horse faltered. He lashed Rosie across the cheek but she was beyond pain. Cheering crowds and faces swept by and then she and Duke were flying down through the center of town and everyone was roaring as Duke found some last reserves and shot across the finish line a good four lengths ahead of the Kentucky horse.

Clint caught her as she tumbled out of the saddle into his arms. "What a race!" he shouted, "I . . ."

The Gunsmith's voice and smile died as he saw the angry red welt across her cheek. He set her down slowly and started to turn and search for Bennie.

"Wait!" she cried, her small voice almost drowned by the noise of the crowd. "Please don't do it. I—I deserve it. Oh, Clint, I took his money and almost let him win. I have to give it back. Please. We won and that's all that counts.''

Clint nodded. He felt anger and betrayal, but she had come out honest in spite of it all and they had won. He took the reins of his horse and walked through the crowd, feeling men slap him on the back with congratulations, hearing the ones that had bet on Duke shout and carry on like happy children.

He walked Duke until the animal cooled down and then he headed out to find William Tippett, the Ft. Worth banker who had his money.

Tippett found him first. ''Here you go, a thousand less the two hundred you borrowed. Nice profit, Clint.''

''Thanks.'' He had to force a smile.

''Say, what in the devil happened out there behind those hills?''

Clint folded the money and shoved it into his Levi's. ''What do you mean?''

''I mean that someone said they saw the girl pull a six-gun out of a cowboy's holster and then almost kill that ugly little jockey that raced her. And then, she showered him with a wad of fifty dollar bills that set off the biggest brawl Ft. Worth has ever seen. Everybody dove for that money and they like to tore each other to shreds.''

A slow grin tugged at the corners of Clint's mouth. He could almost picture Lockerel and Bennie fighting a gang of cowboys for that kind of money. ''What about the girl?''

''I don't know. She just disappeared in the crowd. What's going on?''

Clint handed the reins to Tippett. ''Take him back to the stable, will you? Have him rubbed down and grained when he cools. I had better find her before she does something crazy.''

Clint found Rosie at the stageline office. She had used the last few dollars she owned to buy a ticket to El Paso. Clint tore up the ticket and took her out to dinner and then to bed.

He figured everyone was entitled to mess up once in awhile.

SEVEN

For almost a week, things settled back to normal in Clint's life. A lot of the cowboys left with their herds and the town actually got kind of quiet. Clint hadn't helped Rosie find an "exciting" job yet, but then he hadn't looked very hard either. They were having too much fun and with the money they'd won on the horse race, it just did not seem too all-fired important to get Rosie employment.

Besides, she was obviously kind of fussy. When you ruled out working in offices, cafés, saloons and doing laundry, what else respectable was there for a girl like her to do besides marry? Maybe, Clint thought, Rosie could figure out some kind of legitimate business that she would be interested in starting. Something where a woman could make some real good money and still have a lot of fun doing it.

They were up in the hotel room one morning about ten, just fooling around in bed and talking about this when, suddenly, gunfire erupted down in the street below.

"What's that!" Rosie exclaimed.

Clint jumped out of bed and raced to the window. Down in the street, he saw William Tippett explode out of the bank and heard him shout, "It's a bank robbery! Help!"

Then a small man Clint had not noticed at first glance but who was obviously holding horses for his outlaw friends, opened fire on the banker. Tippett died in mid-stride.

"Jesus Christ!" Clint swore murderously. "That's that little jockey, Bennie! He shot my friend the banker!"

Another short, overweight man wearing a bandana came pounding outside with a satchel of money in his fist.

"It's Lockerel!" Clint shouted for it would be impossible not to recognize him. "Throw me my gun, Rosie! Quick!"

She was a step ahead of him. Rosie was stark naked but that did not slow her down even a little bit. She tossed the Gunsmith his Colt .45 even as chaos reigned in the street below. Men and women were shouting and racing for safety. Clint heard two more shots in the bank and then he had the six-gun in his fist.

Bennie had the outlaws' horses. Crimson Victory, however, was making his life miserable. The stallion reared and was going crazy in the excitement. But Bennie was a horseman of the highest order. Somehow, he did manage to control the thoroughbred and the other three fidgety horses he was holding for his accomplices.

Had Sam Lockerel been a young horseman of equal ability, he would have leapt into the saddle. But he was older and slower and when Clint shot Bennie off his horse, Lockerel and the two other bank robbers who followed close behind were suddenly afoot as their horses stampeded wildly down the main street of town.

"We got them now!" Clint said, just as someone below him opened fire with a shotgun.

Lockerel's corpulent body was lifted over the hitching rail to crash into a horse watering trough. He lay face underwater and unmoving, half in the water and half out.

The other two outlaws bolted back into the Ft. Worth bank and slammed the doors as a hail of bullets came their direction.

Clint expelled a deep breath and turned back from the window to get dressed. "What we have now," he said, no longer in any hurry, "is the makings of a siege."

Time proved him correct. The bank robbers barricaded themselves in their fortified rock building and refused to come out or even to respond except with a smattering of gunfire. It was determined that there were at least three customers and two other employees inside and that fretted people.

Everyone knew that they could all die of thirst. You could go without food for a week and still keep yourself together, but in hot, humid weather, three or four days without water and you would go out of your mind.

Despite the obvious need for patience, there were still a few hotheaded men who wanted to rush the bank and get themselves killed. But Clint argued strongly against a direct attack. It just was not necessary. The place was surrounded day and night. "Give 'em time and this heat," he cautioned. "Mr. Tippett is dead, that's enough good men."

So a couple of dumb cowboys and would-be heroes grumbled, but they waited. The town held a nice big funeral service for William Tippett and it was well attended. The Reverend Bertram gave a stirring sermon and they all sang gospel songs around the grave. Tippett's widow was young and pretty. There were a lot of over-eager jaspers fawning over her and it sort of made Clint ill to see the vultures moving in on the banker's woman before he was even cooled down to the good earth's temperature.

After the funeral, they went back to town and waited out one more blistering day. Some men drank too much and got crazy enough to fire a few random shots at the bank, but it was all bluff and smoke. Clint and the town sheriff told them to stop acting like fools before a stray bullet killed someone innocent inside.

On the fourth day, the bank robbers stuck a rifle barrel out the window and waved a white flag.

"They want to talk," Clint said.

The Gunsmith was elected to accompany the town sheriff across the street to palaver. The sheriff was an old hand at dealing with outlaws and, as they trudged across the street with sweat rivering down their spines, his advise was a terse, "We promise them anything and give 'em a rope when they surrender."

Clint was about to remind the lawman that a trial would come first, though there was little doubt as to a verdict. His words, however, were cut short when a voice from the bank cried, "That's far enough. Hold it right there and listen."

"You're a woman?" Clint asked, hardly believing his eyes when he saw an extremely handsome lady of about thirty standing weakly beside the door with a gun in her fist.

"Yeah, I'm afraid so," she said. "It's me and my little sister Maggie is all that is left of the gang. I don't mind hanging, but Maggie isn't at fault and is only seventeen.''

''That's old enough to know what she was doing,'' the sheriff said bluntly. ''I want the hostages.''

The woman didn't seem to hear him. ''My name is Miss Lola Perdue and I am mightily sorry for the death of the banker. None of it was planned and we'd never have done this if we knew it would all come to such a sad end.''

''Save it for a jury, Miss Perdue,'' the sheriff snarled.

''That's what I want to talk to you about before we give ourselves and these poor people up. I want your word that there will be no lynch party. I want a fair trial for me and my sister. We have some things that we need to say.''

''I'll bet,'' Clint said cryptically.

''You'll get a fair trial,'' the sheriff said grudgingly. ''There will be no lynching in Ft. Worth while Bert Fox is its elected sheriff.''   .

Lola Perdue smiled wanly. ''Your word is good enough for me, Mr. Fox,'' she said, pitching her gun out. ''Now get a doctor and some water and help us with these poor people. We found a bottle of whiskey and another of rye in the bank's meeting room. But you can't drink that stuff all the time when it's so warm.''

''So that's how you lasted four days,'' Clint said.

Lola nodded and stepped back, opening the door wide. She smiled but stiffened suddenly as some fool across the street opened fire with a Winchester and sent a bullet through her upper arm. Lola fell soundlessly. Her young sister cried out and threw herself on the floor while Clint hit the boardwalk lest a stray bullet take his life.

''Goddammit, hold your fire!'' the sheriff yelled, ''You shot a woman!''

Angry voices erupted from the saloon and Clint heard the crash of glass and then an inert body come flying through the window. There would be no more shooting.

Things would settle until the trial. The outlaws being women were going to take the steam out of a lot of men who had talked lynching. For some reason men figured it was justice to swing another man, but their delicate stomachs and standards would not allow that to happen to a woman guilty of the exact same crime. Especially not as pretty a woman as Miss Lola Perdue nor one as young and innocent looking as Maggie, who now lay sobbing on the floor.

Clint studied the pair and found himself unmoved to pity. These two were bank robbers and it was that simple. William Tippett had died partly because of these two women even though he had actually been shot by Bennie.

"Sheriff," the Gunsmith said, "why don't you get this pair to your jail? I'll organize things here and help the others."

The sheriff nodded. "Get up, Miss Perdue," he said roughly. "We can't help you on the floor."

Maggie looked up at him. "You brute!" she cried, "my sister was forced into this. We are no more guilty than those other people inside!"

Clint shook his head. "Miss," he said, "I think you better do your tall talking to a lawyer. Now, do as the sheriff says and help your sister to her feet."

The girl glared at him but she helped Lola Perdue up and, clutching one another as if *they* had been the hostages, the pair of bank robbers allowed themselves to be led to jail.

EIGHT

Clint heard a sharp whistle and turned to stare across the street. Sheriff Bert Fox was sitting on the edge of the boardwalk with a stick and a knife. There was a pile of wood slivers at his feet that gave evidence to the fact that he had been waiting outside of his office for at least a couple of hours.

The sheriff motioned Clint to join him. When the Gunsmith sat down beside the lawman, Fox said, "I wanted to ask you if you ever had women for prisoners."

Clint rubbed his jaw and then nodded. "A couple of times I had to arrest some women of the night that were drugging cowboys with laudanum and then robbing them."

"But they was just whores. I mean, have you ever had any women the likes of the two I got in there?"

Clint did not have to think twice. "Nope. Why do you ask?"

"Because they're creating all sorts of hell inside. Dammit, take a good look!"

Clint stood up and peered through the sheriff's office window. He could not see Lola Perdue or Maggie because of a crowd of attentive women. "What are they doin' in there?"

"Jawin'." The sheriff slashed furiously at his whittle stick. "Those damn women are telling their sad tale of woe to anyone and everyone that will listen. Yesterday, they had a reporter in here and he practically came out bawling, he felt so bad for them."

"That's hard to believe."

"Is it? Then go on inside. Take your place in line and grab a damn crying towel like the rest. I tell you, that Perdue woman could charm snakes or even talk the hump-water out the side of a camel's back. I never seen the likes of her!"

Clint frowned. He had seen some mighty fast talking outlaws, men who would have been much better suited peddling than robbing. "Well," he said, "they sure can't deny they were part of the gang. And the gang killed poor William Tippett."

"But they didn't." The sheriff looked disgusted. "You mark my words, Gunsmith. Tomorrow in the newspaper, their story will be told in such a pathetic manner that the whole town will be wheezin' and sneezin' with sympathy. I'm afraid, if I don't shut that woman up, there will not be enough clear-thinking people in all of Ft. Worth to make an honest jury."

"Oh, now come on!"

"I mean it! According to those two, they are victims of circumstances beyond their control. Yeah, that's exactly how that Perdue woman put it to me last night." Fox looked up from his whittle stick and a slow smile lit his face. He winked and clucked his tongue. "But that sure is a good looking woman!"

Clint nodded. "Very. She been sweet-talking you too?"

"Hell no!" the sheriff protested. "Oh, she sure

tried, but I told her she was wasting her breath. As far as I was concerned, she and her little kid sister were as guilty as sin. I said I expected them to go to prison for life.''

"You said that?''

"Well," the sheriff hedged, "maybe not life sentences. But a few years anyway. There are extenuating circumstances over which they were sorta victims.''

"Like what?''

"Like they were forced into the robbery against their will.''

Clint scowled. He could not believe he was hearing this from a veteran lawman like Bert Fox. "How can anybody force anyone into robbing a bank?''

"Lockerel and that scary little jockey beat them up and threatened their lives . . . and the life of their mother!''

"No.''

"Yes!'' The sheriff shook his head sadly. "If you thought someone was going to kill your mother if you didn't help them, wouldn't you think twice about it?''

Clint figured he'd have to think on that awhile.

"Who's in there right now?'' he asked, standing up again to look inside.

"About every important woman in town," Fox said. "Including . . . I'm warning you. You won't believe this, Gunsmith.''

"Try me.''

"All right. Including Judge Amos Heston's wife, Clarabel.''

"The judge's wife is in there!''

"Yep. She's that big, loudmouthed woman in the white dress with the stupid looking blue bonnet on her head. "See her?''

"Yeah.'' Clint frowned. "Isn't that . . . it's Rosie!''

"Sure it is." The sheriff looked up from his whittle stick and grinned maliciously. "You mean to say that that little honey of yours didn't tell you she was coming over here to join Lola's court of bleeding-heart ladies?"

"No, but then I have never held a tether rope on any woman. They don't ask me where I go and when, and I don't ask them."

"Well, now you know. You wait around and pretty quick you're going to see a bunch of them come out and start asking me for things."

"What things?"

"Wait and see."

That was all Sheriff Bert Fox would say and the Gunsmith did not press the man. So he waited and it was not a half hour later that the group of ladies came outside and stood with their hands on their hips.

Mrs. Clarabel Heston was a big, heavy-boned lady who wore lovely dresses and expensive jewelry. Her hair was gray and she had big sunspots on her hands and arms but she looked as if she could heft barrels of horseshoes. "Sheriff! We demand to speak to you about the welfare of those two poor women you have in your cells."

"Yes, ma'am," Fox said, folding up his pocket-knife and putting it into his vest. He sat what remained of his good, white whittling stick down carefully and then stood up to face the ladies. "What would you like to say, Mrs. Heston."

"We would all like to protest the filth and wretched condition of both cells. We want them cleaned up at once."

"Just mopped 'em out last week. Don't guess they are all that dirty yet."

"But they are! I saw a cockroach in Miss Perdue's cell!" The judge's wife made a terrible face. "A filthy, disgusting cockroach, Mr. Fox."

"Hmmmm. She stomp him?"

Clarabel recoiled with shock and dismay. The response was not the one she had hoped for and expected. "Why no!"

Another woman who looked to be of Clarabel's stature and social position said with a great effort at exerting patience, "Sheriff Fox. We understand that you are not . . . how shall I say this ladies?"

"Not very cleanly," Rosie said.

Fox colored but Clarabel cut off his protest. "Yes, that is it exactly, my dear girl. Now, Mr. Fox, we will volunteer to clean out that cell, put up curtains and—"

"Curtains!" Fox roared. "What in blazes do you think this is, a resort hotel!"

"You do not have to shout!" Clarabel yelled. "We expect those ladies to have decent living arrangements."

"And food."

Fox was turning purple. "You know that our city fathers, in their infinite generosity only allow me two bits a day to feed each prisoner. I won't pay for it out of my own pocket. No sir!"

"Then I would expect that you will not object to our bringing additional food. Pies and cakes, cookies and fried chicken."

Clint would have smiled if Rosie hadn't been standing amongst them. He felt sorry for the sheriff. "Ladies, I'm sure Sheriff Fox appreciates your concern. However, there are rules that need to be maintained for the safety and security of the population as well as the prisoners."

"Poppycock!" Clarabel snapped. "Absolute poppycock! We shall be back with cleaning supplies and nourishment for those two unfortunate ladies."

They all nodded. Even Rosie. And then they marched off.

"See what I meant?" the sheriff crabbed as he sagged back to his original position and unfolded his knife.

Clint nodded morosely. He was surprised and disappointed to see that Rosie had been drawn into the Perdue woman's sugary web of lies. He would have to have a good, heart-to-heart talk with Rosie and straighten out her faulty thinking.

Rosie was angry. She stood in front of the hotel and watched the crowd as it filed into the courthouse to witness what promised to be a fascinating trial. "Clint," she said, "I know you think I am being a silly, sentimental and gullible fool, but I believe that woman and her poor little sister. They were forced into a life of crime. Their entire lives have been a misfortune. Sending them to wither away in prison would be an injustice and a travesty of the law."

"Are you sure of that?" Clint demanded. "What would you say if I told you that I recall hearing about a woman who perfectly fits Miss Perdue's description? The only difference is that Miss Perdue is a blonde like you while the woman I saw on a wanted poster had brown or black hair."

"See! Then it cannot be the same woman."

"Of course it can. Miss Perdue has obviously bleached her hair. Anyone can see that."

"So what! She is innocent." Rosie lowered her voice and gave Clint a quick kiss on the cheek. "I am a woman and women cannot lie to other women. No sir. It never works. We can tell whether or not another woman is lying to us every time."

Clint did not believe that one little bit. "Poppycock!" he said, echoing Clarabel Heston.

Rosie shook her head and sighed. "All right. I tried. Why don't we let the jury decide who is guilty and who is not? It's their job, not ours."

"Good idea. But I have to testify this morning and
if I am asked my opinion, I'll tell the court that I
believe Miss Perdue is a professional storyteller of
the highest order. And a hardened criminal."

Rosie looked miffed. "And what about poor little
Maggie? Is she a hardened criminal, too, at only
seventeen? Should she go to the gallows and swing?"

Clint shook his head. He was tired of arguing.
"Let's go," he said. "The sooner this trial is over
and the sentence is given, the better off we'll all be.
The whole town has gone daft."

"Mercy is the sword of the just," Rosie declared.

"I read that in the Bible too."

"It's not from the Bible," she said triumphantly,
"but it ought to be. *I* made it up."

Clint grumbled and followed the woman into the
courthouse. He was dead certain that Miss Lola Perdue and her poor little sister were going to split Ft.
Worth like the blade of an axe.

NINE

The newspaper article was the most biased piece of journalistic nonsense that Clint had ever read. In it, the reporter endlessly, slavishly quoted Miss Perdue in such a way as to make it sound like mankind in general should be on trial instead of her and her poor sister. Clint actually saw women read it on the street and burst into sympathetic tears. Rosie reread the damned thing so many times she nearly memorized it. And yet, Lola Perdue would not fully disclose either her background or the nature of her upcoming defense, only enough to hint at her previous, grievous circumstances.

"The full story is tragic," Rosie would say over and over. "You haven't heard anything yet."

Clint clamped his teeth together and remained silent. It was clear that public sentiment was swinging in favor of the two women, and that was surprising because frontier justice was usually so merciless.

As to his recollection of a wanted poster, he sent a half-dozen telegrams to various law officials in Colorado, Arizona, Wyoming and Montana but the ones

who responded at all did so negatively. Clint decided
he should have realized nothing would come of his
inquiries. The memory of the woman he sought was
too old, too fragmented and he had given his lawmen
friends almost nothing to go on.

For days, the only topic of interest in old Ft.
Worth was the trial and when the day finally arrived
to begin, the whole town breathed a collective sigh of
anticipation. And when Clint and Rosie entered the
packed courtroom, they were given special attention
because of their involvement.

The jury was seated on the left-hand side of the
courtroom and looked to the Gunsmith to be a good
cross section of Ft. Worth citizenry. There were common laborers, a retired doctor, three housewives and
two of the town's more prominent merchants. All of
them had been selected on the basis of careful questioning.

Clint, being scheduled as the very first witness to
take the stand, was led by the bailiff to a small table
and before he could take a seat, the bailiff stiffened
and said, "Oyez! Oyez! The United States Court of
the State of Texas is now in session. The Honorable
Judge Amos H. Heston is presiding. God bless the
United States of America and this honorable court!"

Judge Heston was an impressive looking man. He
stood six feet tall and had muttonchop side-whiskers
and a silver mane. Clear eyed and strong jawed, he
looked to be a man of his own mind as he strode purposefully into the room dressed in his long, flowing
black robes. As soon as he had taken his seat, he
slammed his gavel down hard and the courtroom fell
silent. "This court is now in session. Bailiff, you may
usher in the accused prisoners and read the charges
against them to the court."

The bailiff dashed into the next room and, with a
hundred spectators leaning forward craning their

necks eagerly to see, he led in Miss Perdue and her
sister and brought them to stand before the bench.
Miss Perdue looked as if she had stepped off the
pages of a fashion magazine. Her hair was beautifully done up and she looked bright and well rested.
Maggie, however, appeared haggard and drawn. Her
eyes were shadowed and they darted around the
courtroom like those of a small, wild animal desper-
ately seeking escape.

"The charges, Your Honor, are the willful act to
commit a bank robbery. During such act, one Mr.
William Tippett, the Manager and Vice President of
the Ft. Worth Bank was murdered. In addition to the
robbery attempt, individuals were also held hostage
against their will during a four day siege. The formal
charges are bank robbery, murder and kidnapping,
Your Honor.''

The judge banged his gavel down hard and silenced
a buzzing of voices in the courtroom. He looked at
the two prisoners and the stiffness in his face disappeared. "Miss Perdue, Miss . . .''

"Perdue also, Your Honor. We are sisters.''

"Thank you,'' the judge said. "How do you both
plead to the charges?''

"Not guilty!'' Lola said lifting her chin proudly.

"Not guilty,'' Maggie whispered, unwilling to look
up at the judge.

"Yes. So I suspected. Very well, please be seated
and let the trial begin with a calling of the first
witness, Mr. Clinton Adams.''

Clint stood up. He allowed the bailiff to swear him
in and then he took the stand as the prosecutor began
his questioning. "Mr. Adams. Is it true that you have
been a distinguished lawman for many years?''

"I have been a lawman. I think the word 'distinguished' might be an embellishment.''

"Don't be modest, sir. You are famous and known

everywhere as The Gunsmith. And did you not, at approximately ten o'clock on Wednesday morning, June the third, see the holdup in progress?''

"I did.''

"Would you please tell us exactly what you saw, leaving out nothing.''

Clint recounted everything except what he and Rosie had been doing at the time. He had testified hundreds of times at trials like this and the questions were almost a routine.

"Then it was you who killed the horse holder, the one named Bennie?''

"Yes.''

"But not the man named Samuel Lockerel?''

"No. Someone got him with a shotgun.''

"It was me and it felt good!'' a burly merchant shouted with an upraised and clenched fist.

His declaration brought cheers and applause and required the judge to pound his gavel. "Silence in this court! Another such outburst and I will empty this courtroom of spectators!''

The room grew very still. Judge Heston had done this before and they knew it was not an idle threat.

The prosecutor turned back to Clint. "Is there any doubt in your mind that the two accused women were in cahoots with the two men you saw killed?''

"None whatsoever,'' Clint replied.

"Then they were definitely part of the hold-up gang.''

"That's what I said.''

"Thank you. And did you see any evidence that the two women were being coerced into participating in the robbery?''

"No. But I never saw them at all until the shooting was over.''

"Thank you. Do you believe the two accused will-fully, and of their own volition engaged in the crimes for which they are accused?"

"Objection, Your Honor!" the defense attorney called out. Such a question is clearly supposition and prejudicial to the jury. Mr. Adams is an expert lawman, but he is not an expert mindreader."

"Objection sustained," Judge Heston said. "If you have no more questions of Mr. Adams, we shall move on to the next witness."

The prosecutor nodded. Clint was excused and then followed by a succession of witnesses. Each one of them had little more to add to what Clint had said but their testimony took all day. At five o'clock, a weary court, jury and crowd of spectators filed out and the two prisoners were taken back to their jail.

There were more of the same questions on the morning of the second day, but no one paid much attention until after the noon meal break when Miss Perdue was finally called to the witness stand.

She was wearing a subdued but very attractive dress which highlighted her hourglass figure and yet managed to convey a high degree of modesty. She looked like the wife of the most handsome and successful man in Ft. Worth.

The judge studied her closely and he smiled. The defense attorney moved over before the accused and cleared his throat loudly. He was young and refined, a peacock of a man if Clint did not miss in judgment.

"Miss Perdue," the young attorney began smoothly, "you have heard a great deal of testimony, all of which basically establishes that you and your sister appeared to be under no duress or threat at the time of the robbery. And yet, it is obvious that you believe your own innocence. Will you, in your own words tell this court why you should not be found guilty as charged."

After she was sworn in, Lola took the stand. She smiled timidly and then swallowed loud enough to be heard in the farthest recesses of the courtroom where absolute silence reigned supreme. "Your Honor, dear jurors, friends, and the dear aggrieved widow of Mr. Tippett whom I shall never ever forget or forgive myself for knowing. Better I had taken that bullet than Mr. Tippett. You cannot begin to know the depth of my remorse, the infinite caverns of my sorrow. But I shall tell you this story of mine—and of poor Maggie—in its brutal entirety leaving nothing out and then let you decide if we are guilty as accused, or simply pawns in the game of life's misfortunes."

Clint groaned. "Get out the crying towels. This is going to be a real gully washer."

Rosie jabbed him painfully hard in the ribs. The courtroom leaned forward, every face etched with a yearning need to understand and to sympathize.

"We were born of a poverty in Westchester County, Virginia so severe we never knew the meaning of Christmas, or that children received birthday presents. Or that there was any beauty at all in this world. Our mother vanished during the winter of 1847; she explained that she had gone to die and she left me a pork rind, a pound of corn and a ribbon. In her letter, she begged, 'Take care of Maggie. I fear for you both.'"

A woman in the room began to sob so loudly that she had to be escorted from the room.

"I tried to take care of my sister. My father, Isaac, he worked us like Missouri mules. Seven days a week. Daybreak to dusk. We never saw another child, or a smile, or any kindness. My father was a hard, unforgiving man. A brutal, twisted man. When I became of age, he . . ."

Lola covered her face and her shoulders began to tremble as she bowed her head. Clint saw tears coursing down Rosie's cheek when she turned to him and whispered, "This next part, it'll tear your livin' guts out."

"I'm sure it will," Clint said, shifting uncomfortably on the hard wooden bench.

"Forgive me," Lola said, wiping her face and trying a smile so painful that even Clint had to look away. "But my father . . . he took me and he . . . used me as a woman until I was eighteen years old and then he went to little Maggie."

The courtroom erupted in outrage and it took the judge five minutes to restore quiet enough for the witness to continue.

"I had no one to talk to. No one to ask for help in the demented world we called home. But I knew my father's taking of little Maggie every night was wrong. Terribly, terribly wrong. Maggie began to scream. She had horrible nightmares and I realized I had to get away before my father hurt us anymore. So we ran away. But I was with child. I didn't even know how such a thing could happen."

The courtroom hummed as men and women shook their heads and swore at the faceless Mr. Perdue, God curse his vile soul!

"My baby was . . . was born dead. It was as if I was being punished for the sin against God that I only then realized I had committed. And what about Maggie? She continued to have nightmares and still does to this day. We came to the West in rags. And I allowed myself to be . . . to be used by many men in order to keep ourselves fed. But I never let another touch dear Maggie."

Lola Purdue choked, her hands knotted at her breasts and she shook her head violently as if she could rid herself of the memories. "Never! But misfortune returned and the man I married was killed by Indians up in Montana. We came south and met Mr. Lockerel and that hideous little jockey two years ago.

They took us in and used us as shills for their betting and evil skulduggery. We doped horses and riders. Had not Mr. Adams and dear Rosalie slept with their black gelding, we would have fixed that great horse so that it could not win over Crimson Victory. Yes, we had gone that low, my poor Maggie and I.''

The judge tapped his gavel down softly. "Miss Perdue. This testimony is extraordinarily painful for all of us. Would you like to continue it tomorrow when you are stronger?''

She shook her head emphatically. "No, please! I cannot bear to wait another minute to complete this tale of pitiless misfortune. I am almost finished. I rebelled against Samuel Lockerel and declared that neither I nor my dear sister would work for him another moment. I should not have done this.''

Lola fell silent. She looked over at Maggie. "Can you stand this last, most terrible confession?''

Maggie, her face stark and pale, nodded.

"You brave, brave girl," Lola whispered reverently before turning back to face the judge and jury.

"Sam Lockerel beat us half to death and then, then he told me that he had discovered that our mother had not died at all but had recovered and fled to North Carolina. Imagine our joy! But then, if you can, our horror when he explained that my mother was living in an insane asylum and that he would have her poisoned to death if we did not help him rob the Ft. Worth Bank.''

The judge blew his nose loudly. He shook his head and hissed, "The maggot-eating scoundrel!''

"Yes," Lola said. "And so we did the terrible deed and now we have come to this sad end. I have no more to say, except that our entire lives have been spent in misery beyond ordinary imagination.''

She looked to the jury. "Will you either hang us and end this cruel charade of life we can no longer endure, or will you free us. We cannot live our lives behind bars. We would die . . . we are already very close to death. In the immortal words of Patrick Henry, 'Give us liberty, or give us death!' " she cried.

There was not a dry eye in the courtroom when Lola Perdue bowed her head in prayer. Not even those of the Gunsmith.

Court was dismissed. There were no more witnesses. No further testimony. Tomorrow, the jury would surely render a verdict of guilty but under circumstances that would require a merciful sentence, maybe even a full pardon.

TEN

That evening, Clint strolled down to the telegraph office with the half-hearted idea of sending off a telegram to a marshal over in Sante Fe, New Mexico who might have heard something about Lola Perdue, or whatever her real name was.

"Mr. Adams," the telegraph operator said in greeting, "I was just about to send a messenger boy to you with this telegram from Dodge City."

Clint took the telegram and read it almost at a glance: LOLA PERDUE WOMAN FITS DESCRIPTION OF KNOWN MURDERESS STOP NEED FURTHER DETAILS ON PAST AND PRESENT CIRCUMSTANCES STOP WILL STIR THE POT AT THIS END SOME MORE STOP AND GOOD LUCK STOP ACE ROBINSON

Clint nodded with satisfaction. He turned and headed out the door. He was going to have a few things to say tomorrow in court.

"Your Honor," he said the next morning after the

bailiff had seated the judge and jury. "I would like to present something to the court."

"Mr. Adams, you may proceed with whatever you have in mind."

Clint turned to address the jury. "Ladies and gentlemen. Ever since I first set eyes on Miss Perdue, I have had a sneaking hunch that I have seen her picture somewhere before. And I think it has been on a federal wanted poster."

The courtroom erupted in anger. Clarabel Heston was among the most vocal as the judge banged his gavel repeatedly and shouted, "Order! Order in my court! Bailiff, I order you to physically remove the next person who opens his or her mouth without my permission. That includes you, Mrs. Heston!"

Clarabel's puffy cheeks flamed but she held her tongue. Even so, everyone knew that the judge was going to catch hell this night.

"Please continue, Mr. Adams. But I warn you, mere supposition is no excuse for slander and innuendo."

"No, Your Honor. I just think that you and the jury shouldn't be so almighty quick to accept that woman's tale of woe. I sent telegrams out and this one," he said, handing it to the judge, "indicates I might have hit on something you need to know."

The judge read it very quickly to himself and then aloud to the jury. When the word "murderess" was spoken, the silence was so intense you could have heard a pin drop.

"Well," the judge said, "this might be a reason to delay sentencing, but I can't, in good conscience, ask the jury to reconvene at a later date. No, I cannot. They have heard the evidence and this telegram, while sobering, is inconclusive and therefore inadmissable evidence."

The judge looked at Lola Perdue. "Miss Perdue, I do not wish to inflict upon you the ordeal of taking the witness stand again. Nevertheless, I must ask if you have any knowledge of what this Marshal Robinson is getting at?"

"No, Your Honor!" Lola looked stricken. "I have never even been in Sante Fe! I and my dear sister are almost rendered speechless."

"I see." The judge pounded his gavel. "I ask the court to dismiss this telegram from its mind and reach a verdict."

The jury filed out. The crowd took a recess and moved into the street. Clint felt like a leper. Only Rosie came over to him and she was furious. "How could you do that!" she hissed. "How could you take a flimsy piece of . . . of nothing and present it to the court! It has cast a doubt upon that poor woman and her sister that could get them hung."

Clint was getting annoyed. "The hell it has!" he groused. "All I did was let them know that maybe Miss Perdue and her sister are telling the truth, but maybe also that woman is the greatest con artist and sinner since Jezebel!"

Rosie made a strangled, angry sound in her throat. She tossed her head, then whirled to stomp away and join the other women.

"You sure created a stir in there this morning," Sheriff Fox said, "I guess you made a few enemies and lost yourself a girlfriend in the process."

"I guess so," Clint said tightly. "I just have this nagging feeling we are being flamboozled. Am I the only one who thinks that way?"

"Yep. I'm sold and I am one suspicious son of a bitch, Gunsmith. No one could put on an act like that."

"Don't be so sure. I just hope that the jury does its

duty and at least gives them a few years in prison.
There can be a hundred good reasons for committing
a crime, but that don't change the fact that you are
still guilty as sin.''

"You're a hard man.''

"No I'm not," Clint said, walking away to stand
alone and wait the jury. "I just don't appreciate
being duped.''

Two hours later, the jury filed in and the courtroom was packed and anxious for the verdict. Judge
Heston banged his gavel and asked, "Has the jury
reached a unanimous decision?''

"We have, Your Honor.''

"Please face the court and announce your verdict
so that all can hear.''

"We find the defendants both guilty of bank robbery. Not guilty of murder. And just a little guilty of
kidnapping.''

The judge's massive brows furrowed peevishly.
"They can't be 'just a little guilty,' Walter. They
either are or they aren't. Now, which is it?''

"Not guilty, then. I mean, those ladies did not take
their prisoners anywhere. They just kept them where
they found them.''

The judge shook his head, indicating that the
jury's logic seemed shot to hell. "So, we have guilty
on bank robbery. What is the sentence?''

Walter glanced around the jury box and then he
pulled out a piece of paper and read a decision which
had obviously been written and rewritten several
times.

"We the jury, find the defendants guilty of bank
robbery and sentence them to one year in the Texas
State Prison.''

The spectators roared with disapproval. Men stood
up on their chairs and shouted in anger.

"Silence!" the judge yelled. "Bailiff, clear this courtroom at once!"

Clint moved outside with the furious crowd and Rosie brushed on past without even glancing at him. The hell with all of them! Clint thought.

"Mr. Adams?"

He turned to see the banker's widow standing close to him. Clint removed his Stetson. "Mrs. Tippett."

She looked up into his eyes. "I wanted to thank you for putting some reason into this farce. Had it not been for that telegram creating a seed of doubt, the accomplices of my husband's murderer would have gone scot-free."

Clint just nodded. "I wanted them to be held long enough for Marshal Robinson to do some further investigation," he said. "If it proves to be groundless, then maybe they should be set free."

"I don't believe that for a single minute and neither do you," Mrs. Tippett said frankly.

She was dressed in black and that somehow made her even more lovely, as fragile and delicate as a white rose. "My husband was a very good man and he is dead. I thank you for killing his murderer. And now, you have put some measure of justice into this trial."

She managed the briefest of smiles. "I just wanted you to know that my husband considered you to be a very special friend. And so do I. Please do not give up on this lead down in Sante Fe and keep me informed of any new developments."

"I will."

She took a deep breath and let it out slowly. She was a tall, willowy young woman, with black hair and dark eyes. Her skin was very pale and absolutely flawless. To Clint, she had always seemed a little aloof, a little bit regal. But not anymore. "I'll do that, Mrs. Tippett."

"Thank you." She left him standing alone with his hat in his hand. And when he walked back to the hotel, not one man on the street called his name or said a friendly word.

It just went to show that you could be a town hero one day and the town goat the very next.

ELEVEN

Rosie had never been so hurt and confused as she was after the jury's decision to sentence Lola Perdue and her little sister to one year in prison. It was so terribly unfair! And Clint, damn him, if he hadn't brought to court that stupid, libelous telegram that had the audacity to insinuate that poor Lola might be a murderess . . . well, that was the thing that had swayed the jury into coming up with that awful verdict and sentence.

Rosie knew she had no choice but to move out of Clint's room and find some job somewhere washing dishes or waiting on tables. She still loved Clint dearly, but she could not compromise her principles and live with a man who had stabbed her friends in the back.

She found a small room in a dingy house on Beach Street for two bits a day which included one meal. Then, she went to visit poor Lola and Maggie at the jail.

Sheriff Fox greeted her coolly. "So," he said, "you moved out on Clint Adams."

"And what business is that of yours?"

"None, I guess. I just figured that I overestimated your character. The Gunsmith stood up for you and he's the best man you'll ever find. There are a lot of other women in Ft. Worth who would give their best silk stockings to bed down with him."

Rosie's cheeks colored. "I don't have to listen to this!" she said hotly. "I want to see the prisoners."

"Sure. But I need to check your bag first and you'll have to wait for all the others. I'm only letting in one visitor at a time."

"That's outrageous!"

"Maybe, but after that Sante Fe telegram from Ace Robinson, I ain't taking no chances."

"You believed that!"

Sheriff Fox shrugged. "I been a lawman for twenty-one years and I have seen all sorts of things that I wouldn't have believed. I trust nothing and no one. Please wait either in my office or outside. You are after Mrs. Peavy who is after Mrs. Winston and so on. You might have quite a wait."

"I'll wait anyway. How long will they be here?"

"My prisoners?"

"Who else!" Rosie said impatiently.

"They are leaving tomorrow for the federal prison."

"Tomorrow! But . . . why so soon?"

"Prudence," the sheriff said. "The judge and I talked it over and feelings are running so high over this whole thing we decided that the sooner we can get those women out of town, the better. I tell you, I been catchin' hell all day from women and I'd quit if I had to hold those Perdue ladies even one day longer than tomorrow. I just ain't paid enough to take this kind of horseshit."

"Sheriff!"

"Well, I'm sorry, but I ain't," he said truculently.

Rosie went into the sheriff's office and sighed with resignation to see the place filled with women. She smiled at them and then stepped back out for a moment and said, "Save my place in line. I'll be back in a little while."

"No hurry," the sheriff said. "Be at least two hours before you get your turn. Why don't you just write them in care of the prison?"

Rosie flushed with anger but said nothing. The sheriff was a lout and so insensitive a man as to be impossible.

She walked down the street and tried to think of what she could do to support herself. Since moving out of Clint's room, there was little hope that she could expect the Gunsmith to be of any help. That meant she would have to find some drudge job at a barely subsistence wage which would keep her in rags and that crummy little room she had rented.

"Hey, Rosie!"

She turned to see the owner of the Cattleman's Club, one of the nicer saloons and gambling halls. He was prosperous, fortyish and fat with little porcine lips and eyes that should have gone into a swine rather than a human. "Hello, Mr. Walker," she said, without warmth.

"Hi baby!" he said, taking her arm and leaning close enough to foul the air with his rancid breath. "Say, what's this I hear about you and the Gunsmith parting the blankets?"

"News travels fast."

"Then it's true."

"Yes," she answered.

He beamed. "Good! How would you like a new roommate? I'll take you in and you can work in my place."

The idea of living and sleeping with this man was more than repugnant. "No thanks."

"Hey," he said, "what's the matter? I got a great room upstairs. Soft bed. Good food and . . . and I'll even pay you five bucks a week."

"Not interested."

His grip tightened on her arm. "You got a better deal somewhere else?" he asked roughly.

"Let go of me!" she warned.

He let go. "You'll never find a better offer than mine in this town. You'll wind up working in a crib like every other snotty little bitch who thought she had something special between her—"

Rosie hit him right in the mouth. He cried out and covered his face. When he pulled his hands away, they were smeared with blood. "You broke my lip!"

Rosie smiled as she hurried on down the street. But when she rounded a corner and leaned for a moment up against a storefront, she bowed her head and had to fight to keep from crying. She was a nothing. Walker had been right, she would wind up working in a crib and in a few horrible years, she would be used up and ugly—inside and out.

"What am I going to do!" she whispered in desperation.

"All right," the sheriff said to Lola after checking Rosie's handbag. "I'll give you thirty minutes to say good-bye just like I gave all the others. At the end of thirty minutes, I'll bring in the next woman. But at five o'clock, that's it. You leave tomorrow morning at eight and you can wave to the whole damn town on your way out. But I'm tired of all this commotion."

He led Rosie to the cell and closed the door so they could speak in private.

Lola Perdue felt her spirits suddenly take wing. This, she knew, was the Gunsmith's woman, the girl who had shot and killed the young cowboy named Jack Wheeler. This was the girl she had decided could and would help her and Maggie escape.

Lola extended her hand and Rosie took it gratefully. "I'm so sorry about you and Maggie. I can't
believe they are sending you to prison with all those
horrible people."

Lola sighed. Her chin quivered but lifted bravely.
"We'll live. I hope. I just . . . well, I wish the jury
would have given us the death sentence instead of a
prison term as I had asked. Maggie is too fragile to
survive in a jail. I'll try to take care of her but . . ."
She purposefully left the sentence dangling like an ex-
ecutioner's sword over her head.

Lola looked deeply into the girl's eyes. "You've
been crying. For us?"

"Partly." Rosie sniffled. "But partly for myself
because I don't know what end I'll come to here.
Probably, I'll be forced into doing what all girls
without family and reputation have done."

"Don't you dare!" Lola said with maternalistic
fervor. "You are too good, too kind to be a prostitute. Better you were in prison with us than that."

"But what else can I do except menial work which
puts me in bondage to someone for less than a dollar
a day! I need some excitement in my life, Lola. I have
always believed that I was born to do something
special."

"I understand you perfectly," the older woman
said, patting Rosie's arm with encouragement. "I
feel the same way and so does Maggie, though you
can see that it has brought us to our downfall. The
ironic thing about it is that I had finally, after all
these years, accumulated nearly enough money to
buy the wonderful mustanging ranch I always
dreamed about."

"Mustanging ranch?"

"Yes. Say, aren't you a wonderful rider? Of
course you are! How could I possibly have forgotten

that you rode the Gunsmith's black gelding to victory over Lockerel's thoroughbred!''

Lola shook her head as if she were confused. "I guess I have so much on my mind right now I am becoming addled. But anyway, I know a man who has a mustanging ranch in Nevada he is willing to sell, and we were going there right after this."

"How sad!" Rosie cried.

"Yes. It is the opportunity of a lifetime. Imagine racing after wild horses. Bringing them in every night and breaking them. Riding them until they were perfectly safe and suitable for people."

"I not only raced my father's horses as a little girl, but helped train them," Rosie said eagerly.

"Oh," Lola sighed, her eyes seeming to drift clear to Nevada, "You would have been our perfect pardner. What a team we could have made."

"I'll wait for you!" Rosie felt the excitement growing stronger in her. "I mean, I know how terribly long a year would seem in prison, but I'd be willing to work hard and save up some money to buy into the mustanging ranch. Then . . ."

"No, no," Lola said with discouragement. "The ranch is a steal and I fear someone will already have bought it. And by then, dear Maggie's health will be broken. It was just one of those miraculous opportunities that hit once in a lifetime. You either grab it then and there or it is lost to you forever."

Rosie gripped the cell bars and shook them in her helpless rage. "This is so cruel! So unfair to all of us. I would do anything to change this."

"Would you really?" Lola said. "Would you save our lives and ensure our partnership and our futures?"

Rosie looked up suddenly. "Are you asking me to help you escape?" she said in a low voice stretched so thin that it sounded foreign to her own ears.

"Yes!" Lola said dramatically. "There are times when the law errs in tragic ways. Then it is everyone's duty to act according to their conscience. We need your help. Will you give it to us, or shall we suffer cruel injustice, possibly even death? I swear by all that is holy no one will suffer serious injury."

Rosie felt a chill pass through her body. She started to shake her head and then she realized that Lola was right. The law was to protect the innocent, not crucify them in its ignorance. It was her duty to act.

"Tell me how," she whispered. "And I will do it."

"Are you sure? You must be willing to do as I say and act courageously. We need guns and horses, also some food for the race to Mexico."

"Mexico? I thought we were going to buy a mustang ranch in Nevada."

"Of course we are. But first, Mexico. Then, after a few weeks, we go to Nevada to begin our wonderful new life together."

Lola closed her eyes and when she opened them, they were wet with tears. "Rosie, you are a godsend. We'll be so happy together. No more sorrow. Thank you!"

Rosie nodded. "I only have a few minutes left. Tell me exactly what I need to do."

Lola smiled. "You will make a wonderful pardner."

TWELVE

Stealing three horses proved to be easier than expected. Rosie simply waited until just before dawn and then she visited the back lot of The Red Lantern House. It was the best brothel in town, one where women entertained men for the night rather than by the hour. The fact that the horses were all branded was enough to discourage anyone from taking an animal for resale. As a result, men put their animals into a stall, loosened their cinches, and thought nothing of hurrying on inside to sample the fleshy pleasures that awaited.

Getting two pistols was a bit trickier. Rosie pulled one from the holster of a drunken cowboy who lay passed out in an alley. She bought the second gun from a man who had lost everything playing poker and needed the money to pay the feed bill for his horse so he could leave Ft. Worth and catch up with the last trail drive.

Dawn found Rosie waiting just outside of town in a copse of silvery-leafed cottonwood trees. She was nervous, even scared but determined to free Lola and

Maggie. The plan was very simple. She would muss herself up, dirty her face and appear dazed when the special stagecoach carrying the Perdue women and a marshal appeared.

No stage driver would pass a pretty woman in obvious trouble. Then, she would simply allow herself to be placed in the coach where she would pull a gun on the marshal and then help Lola and Maggie bind and gag the poor fellow. It would not be difficult to similarly incapacitate the driver.

The hours dragged by so slowly that it seemed as if she had been waiting all day when she finally saw the roostertail of rising dust. It had to be the coach. Rosie slipped the guns into her skirt pockets.

"This will make me an outlaw," she said to herself, "but I don't care. This is a blow for honest justice. And besides, anything would be better than what awaits me back in Ft. Worth's red light district."

She mussed her long blonde hair and then flopped down in the road and wriggled around in the dirt, careful to rub both cheeks. Then, just before the stagecoach swung into view, she pushed herself up to her hands and knees and pulled her skirt high to reveal her shapely legs.

She was taking no chances.

The driver saw her at once and she heard him yell, "Whoa up there horses!" as he sawed on the lines and brought the coach to a screeching halt not far from where she was positioned.

The driver tied his lines around the brake and leapt down to run to her side. "Ma'am," he yelled, "what happened?"

Rosie slowly lifted her head. Her long blonde tresses hung down around her face and she mumbled, "Horse threw me, I'm hurt."

"Oh Christ!" the driver swore. He was a slender,

nice looking young fellow in his thirties who smelled of horses and leather. When he reached down to pick her up in his arms, she noticed that he was wearing a wedding band. "Don't worry, ma'am, we'll get you to a doctor!"

"Thank you," she murmured weakly.

He had to struggle to pick her up but managed to reach the coach and yelled, "Marshall, we got a hurt woman! Open up in there!"

The door swung open. A bearded, heavyset man glared at her without pity. He had a gun in his meaty fist and when he finally seemed satisfied, he holstered his gun and motioned the driver to shove her in. "What the hell happened to her?"

"Horse took a spill, I'd guess. She's hurt bad! We got to go back to Ft. Worth."

"No! We go on."

"But Marshal, the next town is twenty miles away," the young driver cried. "This lady could die by then!"

"That's her problem," the lawman said as he roughly pulled her inside. "I got my own problems. We keep going."

"But—"

"Godammit! Don't question me!" the marshal snarled. "I don't like having another woman in here to . . ."

He never finished. Rosie didn't even feel Lola Perdue's hand as it slipped into her skirt pocket and pulled out the Colt revolver. Suddenly, there was an explosion of muffled gunfire and the marshal's face went slack.

"No!" Rosie screamed, twisting around. "You said . . ."

The gun boomed between them again and the marshal collapsed with a neat, blue-black hole in the center of his forehead.

Rosie screamed again and threw herself away from the man. When Lola swung the pistol around and aimed it at the driver, Rosie chopped her arm. The gun bucked and fired. The errant bullet struck Maggie in the leg and she howled in pain.

"Damn you!" Lola shouted.

"Run for your life!" Rosie cried in warning as she grabbed Lola Perdue's wrist and fought for the Colt revolver.

The driver probably had a shotgun up beside his seat but that was of no help now and he was not wearing a six-gun. So he did what any man with half an ounce of brains would do, he ran for his life.

Lola swore viciously. She raised her fist and punched Rosie twice but could not wrench the gun free. Maggie was screaming in pain and Rosie bit Lola on the wrist. Bit her until the woman cried out and the six-gun clattered down on the floor between them. They both pitched forward and scrambled for its possession.

Lola won. She wrenched the gun up into Rosie's face and screamed, "Stop it or I'll kill you!"

Rosie, stuffed between the two seats and totally helpless, hissed, "Go ahead. We'll all hang for murder now anyway. Go ahead!"

"You fool!" Lola cried. "The only one who could hang you was that driver and you let him go free! We have to run him down!"

"No," Rosie said. "Let him go. I won't stand for any more murdering!"

"Help me!" Maggie said weakly. "I'm shot!"

Lola dropped the gun and searched the dead marshal's pockets until she found the key to her handcuffs. She quickly unlocked the hated manacles and then she tore a strip of cloth from her dress and yanked up Maggie's dress to her hips. She tied a bandage around the wound and managed to get the blood to slow and then stop.

"Shut up! It's only a flesh wound. You spineless little bitch! We have to get out of here."

Maggie began to cry and Rosie pushed herself out of the coach. She tumbled to the ground and retched until her stomach was empty. Then, she looked up at Lola Perdue and her eyes were filled with hatred. "It was all a lie, wasn't it? Every bit of your testimony. The mustanging ranch, too. Everything you said and did was nothing but a lie."

"I'm an actress. A Shakespearean actress," the woman said as she finished tying her sister's bandage and pulling down her skirt.

Rosie shook her head. "And a murderess. Clint was right. He was the only one in town that you didn't fool."

Lola snickered. "If I'd have been able to get him alone, I'd have made him a slave. Now get up and bring those horses."

"No," Rosie said.

"You can help us escape or I'll leave you to the townspeople. Do you have any idea what they will do to you? They'll know I made fools of them all. You'll never live to reach a courtroom, and the greatest actress in the world could not fool them a second time. They'll hang you from those trees over there."

"I don't care."

Lola climbed out of the stage. She reached down and pulled the Colt along with the derringer from Rosie's pockets. Ignoring Maggie's whimpering, Lola settled on her haunches and said to Rosie, "Have you ever seen a woman hang?"

Rosie shook her head.

"It's terrible. Men stare at her legs and—"

"Stop it!" Rosie screamed as the picture of herself jumping and thrashing at the end of a rope seared her mind. "Stop it!"

"Then you had better help us get away from here. Where are our horses?"

Rosie stared at the cottonwood trees where they would hang her. "Over there."

"Go get them," Lola said, her voice gentling. "We are in this together all the way now. You wanted an exciting line of work, you'll have it. And pretty soon, you'll have money and wonder why you ever did an honest day's work in your life."

Rosie pushed herself to her feet and slowly walked to the horses. It was funny. Because of actions during the last few awful minutes, a life was lost but a life was also saved. The driver had been a married man. Perhaps a father of many children. The marshal had been mean and coldhearted.

As she returned with the stolen horses, Rosie tried to take some small, mind-saving comfort in the thought that she had at least saved the better man.

THIRTEEN

The knocking on his door brought Clint out of bed and reaching for his gun. "Who is it?"

"Telegram for you, Mr. Adams. Another one from Sante Fe. Brought it right over this time."

Clint stepped into his pants and opened the door. The operator handed it to him. "I think you'll find this very interesting."

The Gunsmith felt an edge of hopefulness. "Thanks," he said, reaching into his pocket and then handing the telegrapher a generous tip. "I appreciate your bringing it right over."

He closed the door and walked over to the window where he read the message. LOLA PERDUE FITS DESCRIPTION OF WOMAN WANTED FOR MURDER IN ALBUQUERQUE AND NOGALES STOP WARRANTS FOR HER ARREST FORTHCOMING STOP EXTREMELY DANGEROUS AND MAY HAVE SISTER ACCOMPLICE NAMED MAGGIE STOP ONE THOUSAND DOLLARS REWARD FOR LOLA WHICH WE SHARE STOP ACE ROBINSON

"That's it, then," Clint said with satisfaction. He would go and find the sheriff and ask the man to wire ahead this vital information to the marshal. This would also ensure that they received the thousand dollars reward. Clint would give the sheriff a nice split of his half and still come out with a pretty good hunk of change.

As he dressed and then hurried to find Sheriff Fox, he found himself wondering about Maggie. Was she also a murderess? If so, why wasn't there a reward on her head as well? It did not seem possible and yet, if there was one thing that Clint had learned, it was that you could not know or guess the inner workings of people's minds by their appearance. How many times had he seen a big, strong man run in the face of danger while some bespectacled little bank or mail clerk stood up and fought like a terrier? Courage was like an underground river, it just flowed deep and quiet and you only knew it was there or not when the wells ran dry and you had to reach down deep inside.

He found the sheriff eating breakfast at the Lariat Café and he edged in beside the lawman and ordered coffee.

Fox kept right on eating until he was finished, then he looked at Clint and said, "I assume you have a reason for coming here to interrupt my breakfast."

"I do." Clint took his coffee black. But it was too hot so he blew the smoke off of it for several minutes.

"Well," the sheriff said, finally losing his patience. "What is your reason?"

Clint tested his coffee again. Finding it satisfactory, he took a sip and then handed the telegram to the sheriff who read it with his lips moving over each word.

"Well I'll be damned!" he whispered. "You were right all along."

Clint said nothing. He drank his coffee slowly and when it was all gone he said, "I think you had better telegraph the next town and warn that marshal that he has someone pretty dangerous in custody."

"Think so?" Fox asked skeptically. "That marshal was a tough-looking son of a bitch. I doubt that he will let either of them Perdue woman pull the wool over his eyes."

"I'd still feel better," Clint insisted. "I'd want to be warned if it was me."

"I suppose you're right," the sheriff said, hauling his bulk out of the café booth and heading for the door with a yell, "Put it on my bill, Ellie!"

"I will, Sheriff," the waitress called. She moved over to Clint. "How about some breakfast, Gunsmith?"

"Sure," he said. "The usual steak and eggs."

"More coffee?"

"You bet."

Ellie smiled. She liked the Gunsmith because he tipped big and he had a handsome smile.

Clint was just finishing his breakfast when the sheriff came bustling back into the café and then shoved himself into the booth. He looked shaken.

"I got some real bad news."

Clint set his cup down. "I'm listening."

"Lola Perdue shot the marshal dead and escaped with her sister."

"But how!"

The sheriff expelled a deep breath. "She was helped by Rosie."

Clint stiffened. "I don't believe it!"

"The driver is a witness. He described her right down to that little mole on her cheek and her pretty blonde hair. Height, weight, build, everything. You know there aren't many women as pretty as Rosie or as big upstairs as she is."

Clint stared at his coffee.

The sheriff continued. "We'll search Ft. Worth for her and ask around, but I'll bet you anything she is gone."

Clint stood up. He took a deep breath and let it out slowly. "Where did it all take place this morning?"

"Over near Ryan's Crossing. Can't be ten miles away."

"I know the place." The Gunsmith headed for the door. He needed to read the signs and if the sheriff's words were true, he needed to find Rosie and get her out of this mess before a lynch mob found her first.

Clint rode out of Ft. Worth and let Duke cover the ground in a hurry. He had a bad feeling inside and it ate at him. Rosie was a good girl, not the kind to hook up with a woman like Lola Perdue. But once she had taken the outlaw trail, there was no turning back.

Not ever.

And Rosie wouldn't last on that trail. She was tough—it took a tough woman to have pulled a gun and killed Jack Wheeler—but she wasn't hard. There was a difference and it spelled either destruction or survival among the outlaws and hardened criminals. Rosie was tough, but inside she was marshmallow soft. She wouldn't be able to stand up to the things that she would be forced into seeing or doing.

All the way out to Ryan's Crossing, Clint tried to tell himself that he wasn't at fault. He had warned Rosie that something about Lola Perdue's stirring testimony just did not ring true. But Rosie had been suckered just like the rest of Ft. Worth. Who could blame her? Hell, even an old veteran like Bert Fox had been fooled.

I warned her all I could, the Gunsmith thought. But I should have done something more. He shook his head when he saw the stage and the horses stand-

ing abandoned on the road. He was lucky. So far, no
one had reached the scene of the killing and disturbed
the evidence.

Clint tied Duke to the rear wheel of the wagon.
The door was hanging open and he looked inside to
see the dead marshal. Shot twice, once in the chest,
once in the forehead.

Clint examined the coach in minute detail. He
noted the handcuffs, the marshal's gun still in its
holster. The Gunsmith found more blood on the
floor and studied it because it did not belong to the
marshal. Had Rosie been shot? Or was it Maggie or
even Lola herself. Clint could not tell but the knowledge that one of the trio was at least superficially
wounded was valuable. Once the interior of the
coach had been inspected to his satisfaction, Clint
circled the coach and studied the tracks. He found
where Rosie had lain down in the soft, powdery dirt.
He took a twig and broke it off to her exact boot size.
With a growing sense of depression, he read how the
driver had dismounted, carried Rosie to the coach
and then the rest was clear.

Clint untied Duke and led him over to the cottonwood trees and found the place where three tied
horses had waited for several hours. The ground was
pawed and chewed up, horse manure was plentiful
and so were Rosie's bootprints.

With a heavy heart, Clint mounted Duke and lined
out south to follow the three horses. He wanted to
find Lola Perdue very badly. Maggie, he had no feelings for one way or the other. But Rosie, that was
going to be pure hell.

She even wanted to marry me, he thought savagely, but of course, I turned her down. And look
what that caused. A dead marshal and a good girl
gone bad.

FOURTEEN

It rained that first day on the trail so hard that the Gunsmith found himself seeking shelter under a tree. To make things even worse, instead of clearing in the morning, it rained even harder.

Clint cussed and pulled his sopping Stetson down low over his eyes. The outlaw trail he had followed was gone, totally obliterated by the sleeting rain. He pulled Duke to a halt about noon and surveyed the huge, grassy tableland. The women had started out north, which meant, if Clint read Lola Perdue well, that Lola would change direction. But that still left three choices and Clint had no idea which she might have taken. She could be headed south for the safety of Mexico, or east toward Louisiana and the Mississippi River where the pickings for a pretty woman with a larcenous heart were always good. And she might even be headed for California.

Clint shook his head. He had left in such a damned hurry he had not even taken the time to grab his bedroll or personal gear from his room. So with great reluctance, he turned Duke around and headed back toward Ft. Worth. Only a fool would just start riding without a trail to follow or even a good hunch.

What I need, Clint thought, is some clue as to the woman's intentions. Some hint at which direction she might be moving. He decided he would telegraph Ace Robinson again stating his problem and requesting some background information. He would also telegraph several of his lawmen friends in other towns and ask them to be on the lookout for the three women. Knowing Lola Perdue, she would be getting into some kind of trouble very quickly.

Clint bent his head to the rain and eased his weary horse into a trot. Damn but it galled his pride to lose a trail! But it had happened before and it would probably happen again.

The sheriff was standing in his doorway watching the streets of Ft. Worth turn into a river of mud.

"Gunsmith!" he bellowed. "I want to see you."

Clint nodded. "Soon as I put my horse away and feed him."

The sheriff didn't like the idea of waiting on a horse, but Clint didn't like the idea of having Duke stand out in the rain with an empty belly. So he rode over to the livery and unsaddled the black gelding. He rubbed him down with dry sacking and let the liveryman tie on a feed bag of oats and then pitch him some fresh hay.

Bert Fox was so impatient that he did not wait for Clint but forded the muddy streets and got himself wet and sloppy in the process.

"Dammit, Clint, you sure put a lot of stock in that horse of yours."

"He puts a lot of stock in me," Clint said without humor. "I'm living off his race winnings over Crimson Victory."

"Speaking of which, he's gone."

"Gone?"

"Stolen right out from under our noses last night during the rain. Took him out of the stall down there at the end of this very same barn."

Clint frowned. It couldn't be possible that Lola Perdue had returned for the thoroughbred, could it? And if so, why?

"Want to tell me what you're thinking?" the sheriff asked. "Or am I supposed to be a mind reader?"

"I was just thinking that maybe Lola has the idea of using that red stallion to make money racing same as Lockerel and his jockey, Bennie. Only now, she's fixing to use Rosie as the jockey."

"You think so?"

"I don't know." Clint walked down to the stall and moved inside. Anybody been in here?"

"Only the horse and whoever took it." The sheriff frowned. "I mean, you sure don't have to walk into that bitty stall and search for a stallion to know he's missing."

Clint ignored the sarcasm. He bent and studied the tracks. First, he took out that piece of twig that he had used to measure Rosie's bootprints. She was the horsewoman of the three and she'd be the only one able to get into the stallion's stall and handle the high-spirited animal.

"What the hell are you doing?"

Clint laid the twig down over the best bootprint he could find. Rosie was here! The prints matched perfectly.

"Do you know who did it?" the sheriff demanded impatiently.

"It was Lola all right," Clint said, not wishing to tack on any more crimes to Rosie's name, though he supposed it did not matter. She was already thrice a horse thief.

"Are you sure?"

Clint nodded. He used a piece of straw to carefully measure the stallion's hoof size. There might be a hundred horses with the same size shoe, but sometimes this worked.

"Son of a bitch!" the sheriff groaned. "You mean they came back here in the pouring rain and stole a dead man's horse!"

"That's about the size of it." Clint stood up. "I don't think they started out to do it, but they must have hit on the idea pretty soon after they left the stage. It's a good idea, too. Rosie on that stallion will cause a sensation wherever she goes."

"Good. That'll make it easier to hear about."

Clint agreed. He patted Duke on the shoulder and started for the door.

"Where are you going now?"

Clint stopped. It was still raining and the streets were even sloppier. "Telegraph office. I want to send out the word. Also to see if I can get anymore background on Lola. Might help us to figure out where she's heading."

"Well, this time, keep me informed," the sheriff groused. "I'm the law in Ft. Worth and I didn't appreciate you messin' up the evidence out at the stagecoach."

"Sorry."

The sheriff seemed somewhat mollified. "You . . you learn anything out there?"

"Only that one of the women was wounded."

"How'd you tell that?"

"I saw a bullet hole in the floorboard opposite the marshal's seat. Had to be from his gun."

The sheriff sighed. "Gunsmith, I am starting to

feel like I oughta just hand you this tin badge and go retire to a rocking chair.''

Clint tugged his hat down tight. "Why don't you go check on all the town doctors to see if Lola, Maggie or Rosie came in to have a bullet wound cared for?''

The sheriff blinked. "By God, I think I'll just do that! Fact, I was just thinking I'd do that when you suggested it.''

Clint managed a tight smile. "Of course you were, Sheriff. Keep me posted.''

"By the way.''

Clint stopped in the rain.

"The banker's widow, Mrs. Tippett, she asked if you'd stop by her house.''

"What for?''

"Beats me. She's pretty upset about the Perdue women escaping, and I don't think she has much faith in my ability to find and arrest them.''

Clint moved on through the sloppy mud. He would send the telegrams first and then go see Mrs. Tippett. Afterward, he'd see if the sheriff had learned anything from the doctors and then pass by the telegraph office and check on any replies.

That done, he was going to get himself a steak and a glass of whisky because he had not eaten since yesterday. A man had to feed himself well in this cold, wet weather or he'd get sickly.

And after the meal, he would get a hot bath, a shave and then into some clean, dry clothes and wait until something came back to him. Some news, some piece of critical information that would give him a start in the right direction.

Clint hoped it would not be a long wait; waiting was the thing that he did worst of all.

FIFTEEN

Mrs. Marilyn Tippett lived in a stately two story mid-Victorian home in the best section of Ft. Worth. Clint was really in no mood to visit the widow. He was tired, unshaven, unwashed, mud-splattered and wet. He was also bone tired and hungry. But he had promised the woman that he would keep her up to date on any new developments and when a man gave a lady his word, it was binding.

Clint hardly knew Marilyn at all. He had been to the Tippetts' home once for dinner but the conversation had been formal until he and the banker had moved into a cozy library. There seated in deep leather chairs, they had sipped expensive brandy and enjoyed a cigar and each other's company until almost midnight. William Tippett had been a fine man, son of a banker who had inherited his father's business and continued with the sound, conservative financial practices which had made his father so successful.

Young Tippett's death had been a loss to the entire

community and it was assumed he would have been
the mayor of Ft. Worth in a few years and possibly
even moved into state or national politics. He was
that caliber of gentlemen.

Now, as Clint stood on the wide porch of the
lovely Victorian home and brushed at the mud that
crusted his pant legs, he felt he had made a mistake in
coming here before taking a bath, shaving and
changing into clean, dry clothes.

"Clint," she said, opening the door and smiling.
"You . . . you look a little bedraggled. Come in out
of the rain!"

"I'm afraid that my boots are all muddy. I don't
want to track them across your carpets, Marilyn."

"Then please take off your boots. I really do wish
to speak to you at some length about this terrible Perdue woman business. And . . . and I just need to talk.
To someone. Anyone who will listen.

"You know, being a widow is terrible. Everyone
assumes that you want to mourn in shuttered silence.
Nothing could be farther from the truth. At least for
me. Is that so wrong?"

"Of course not." Clint took off his boots and
placed them outside the door. "No, please bring
them inside and place them before the fire so they'll
be dry when you leave."

"I can't stay long."

"Just for dinner. Please. I have been eating alone
since William died and it is so terribly depressing. Do
you like fried chicken and string beans? Potatoes and
gravy? I have even baked us a rhubarb pie!"

He stepped inside and the sudden warmth made
him shiver violently. He sneezed.

"Bless you! You're wet and freezing to death!"

"No, I—"

"I should be ashamed of myself for being so selfish. Here you are, cold and miserable and I'm prattling on, talking a mile a minute and . . .''

The woman began to shake like a leaf and then, suddenly, she was throwing herself into Clint's arms and crying uncontrollably. Clint held her, knowing his dirty wet clothes would soil her dress but not sure what he could do about it. The woman was obviously hysterical. She needed someone to hold on to and he guessed he was it.

"Please stay for supper," Marilyn whispered. "I'm afraid of being alone right now."

Clint shivered.

She stepped back and wiped her tears away with the back of her hand. She was extraordinarily beautiful. He touched her dress. "I'm afraid I've gotten you all messed up."

"I was already 'all messed up,' Clint. But you must get out of those wet clothes and let me find you some dry things to wear for supper. William's things would fit you perfectly. He was exactly your size, I think.''

"I couldn't—"

"Of course you could. You must. I can't have you sitting at my dinner table shivering and catching pneumonia. Please. Go up and draw a bath and shave, you'll feel better and then we can have something to drink and I'll have supper ready.''

Clint thought about how he had intended to check back at the telegraph office and then the sheriff to see if any of the town's doctors had treated Lola, Maggie or Rosie. But those things could wait a little while. Right now, it was clear that this woman should not be allowed to stay alone.

So he went upstairs and showed him William's bedroom and wardrobe. Clint was surprised that the young banker had slept in a separate room from his wife, but he guessed that when a man had a lot of money and empty rooms, he might do things like that. He shaved with a sterling silver blade and soaked in hot water with a manly scented bath oil that Marilyn pointed out to him. Afterward, he went down to find a beautiful dinner waiting.

"French wine," he said, admiring its bouquet and taste.

"That's all that William drank, but he drank quite a lot of. it sometimes. We have a wine cellar downstairs."

"I see."

"That burgundy smoking jacket was my favorite. William looked very handsome in it, but I must say that you do, too."

"Thank you." Clint raised his glass in a toast and then realized how ridiculous it was because there really was no reason to toast. The woman had just lost her husband and the Perdue women had escaped. Even so, Marilyn raised her glass and said, "To a future."

He nodded and drank, then noticed that her glass was almost empty and refilled it.

"Clint, I want you to know that I believe you are the one man who can find that vile murderess and bring her to justice. I don't expect Bert Fox to be of any value. And besides, he is the town sheriff and is paid to be here, not chasing down to Mexico or wherever the trail may lead."

"Right now, there is no trail." Clint then explained what he had found and how he intended to proceed. "There really is no other way. The rain wiped out the physical tracks and I have to rely on my lawmen network of friends to help."

"That doesn't sound very hopeful."

"The West is big," he said, "but not so big that it

can swallow up or hide a woman like Lola Perdue and her sister forever. Sooner or later they will be seen and in trouble again. They'll either rob a bank or a stagecoach or . . ."

"What about Rosalie? I understand that she and you were . . ."

"We were sharing a room at the hotel," Clint said without batting an eye.

"I see. Then you must have thought very fondly of her."

"I did."

"Would you . . ." Marilyn hesitated.

"Would I what?"

"Bring her to justice."

Clint heaved a sigh. "I don't know. Probably. She is guilty, and I've been a lawman too damn many years to start turning the other way now. I think I'd have to arrest her and bring her in with the others."

"What if she tried to kill you? Would you shoot her?"

Clint set his fork down and his brow furrowed. "Why are you asking me these questions, Marilyn?"

"I don't know. I have been wondering. I would not like you to be killed on the mistaken belief that Rosalie would gladly go to prison rather than use a gun."

"I'll face that bridge when I have to cross it."

"I want to pay you money to help defray your expenses of the hunt," she said. "I want you to take as long as is necessary to find them. And I want all three brought to justice."

"I would do that with or without your money."

"Does your male pride forbid you to take money from a widow? If so, let me tell you this—William left me a very large estate and I am a wealthy woman. I own the bank and many properties around Ft.

Worth. But what I really need is a friend I can trust and a man who will go to the ends of the earth to bring those three to justice.''

"I will be all those things," Clint said, studying the woman closely as she poured them more wine. "But I won't do it for money. I'll do it for many things, but not for money."

She raised her glass to her lips. "I must tell you something. I was very, very fond of William. But I never loved him nor did he love me. He had a woman, I never knew until the funeral which one she was. He loved her, but she was not 'proper enough' to be the wife of a rising young community leader. I felt sorrier for her than I ever did for myself when I saw her grief-stricken face at the funeral. I sent her a thousand dollars anonymously. She earned more than I ever did from him."

Clint shook his head. "I had no idea."

"Neither did anyone else in Ft. Worth. But that is why we had separate bedrooms. We did not have a marriage, we had a partnership."

"I'm sorry."

"Don't be." She sighed. "I was happy. I had all the material things: this lovely home, jewels, furs, trips to New Orleans, San Francisco and New York. William was a very generous man in all things but his love."

Clint shifted in his seat. "Are you trying to tell me that you have not made love all these years?"

"Yes. It never bothered me until I stood beside the grave and realized how quickly life and love passes us by. One day we are young and strong, the next old, alone and feeble. I have missed things in life, Clint. I have missed knowing a man."

"And you want to know me." It was not a question. He could see a fire in her eyes and a hunger that mere food would never satisfy.

"Yes. I want you to hold me all night long and love me so that when you leave, I will feel a part of me come alive that has been too long dead."

Clint blew out a deep breath and shook his head in wonder. "I think . . . he said slowly, "I think you had better get some brandy and a big rug to put before the fireplace. It is going to be a very long night."

She leaned over and kissed him with a passion that was startling in its intensity. "I have so much making up to do," she breathed. "Could we please hurry and get this damned dinner over with?"

Clint laughed and headed for the liquor cabinet for the brandy and glasses. Outside, it was chill and the rain was still falling. But inside, things were heating up fast.

SIXTEEN

The fire crackled hotly as the woman undressed Clint exactly as she might have unwrapped her biggest, most exciting Christmas present. Marilyn Tippett was breathing rapidly and Clint could feel her hands tremble as she unbuttoned his pants and slipped her cool, supple fingers around his swelling manhood.

"Oh my," she whispered, "this is going to be very, very special tonight."

Clint pulled back her flowing silk dressing gown and ran his fingers over her small but very firm breasts. When she closed her eyes, he rubbed her hard nipples and she melted against his body as they kissed.

"We had better lie down in front of the fire before my legs buckle," Marilyn said breathlessly. "I'm not used to this sort of thing, you know."

"I can't believe any man would neglect a woman as beautiful and sensuous as you are," Clint said, pulling her down on the thick, bearskin rug she had placed before the hearth for them.

Marilyn gasped with pleasure as his hands moved across her flat, hard stomach and then passed softly over her silken mass of pubic hair. Clint stroked her softly, wanting this to be especially good for her. When she closed her eyes and began to move her hips provocatively, he slipped his finger into her hot womanhood and she made a small, hurt sound that he knew meant she did not hurt at all. She reached down and pushed his finger in deeper and began to rotate her hips in a slow ellipse even as her right hand worked his stiffening rod.

"I don't think," she said, "that I can wait very long."

"Take your time," he said, kissing her neck, her face, her breasts until she was writhing in ecstasy and he could feel her juices running.

"Oh, Clint, I can't stand this! Please, put it in!"

The truth of the matter was that Clint was already low on self-control himself. He throbbed in her hand and she did not have to ask for him twice. He moved over her, poised and when she grabbed ahold of him fiercely, he drove himself into her slick tunnel of desire.

She raked his back in a frenzy and her hips rotated upward to enclose his entire length. She made small, animal sounds in her throat and her lips drew back from her teeth. "Do it quickly," she begged. "Take me hard!"

Clint felt her long, slender legs wrap around his waist. This woman was like a sleek cat, totally different from Rosalie but every bit as passionate and desirable. She was rippling and hard, she had little padding between her legs and Clint knew he was in her all the way as he began to pump with great enthusiasm.

"Now!" she cried. "Yes, it's happening now!"
Clint slammed into her feeling her body convulse and
her legs jerking around his waist. She was racked by
spasms so powerful that she cried out with joy. She
kept bucking and moaning until finally, she stiffened
and then collapsed to lie spent and drained but smiling.

"You," she said, "have reintroduced me to the
wonder of lovemaking. I had forgotten how fantastic
it really felt. I don't think any man has brought me
higher than you just did."

Clint kissed her eyelids, her nose, her damp cheeks
where tears of happiness had left a shine. He was still
rotating his hips, still working on his own exquisite
and growing fever. Soon, Marilyn's eyes closed and
she clasped him tightly as she began to work her
muscles and milk him greedily.

"Come on, honey," Clint urged through gritted
teeth, "it'll be even better for you the second time!"

Clint gripped the deep fur of the bearskin rug and
drove himself into the beautiful woman with mount-
ing urgency. The fire crackled behind them and their
bodies grew slick with perspiration and the firelight
colored them golden.

"It's coming again!" she panted, "Oh, Clint, here
it . . . comes!"

This time, the Gunsmith could not hold back his
own flood of desire. He slammed into her and his
huge rod spewed seed in great, drenching bursts as he
filled her hot love tunnel. Her legs flailed and she was
lost in a swirl of passion that did not end until she fell
back and almost fainted.

"Oh, Clint," she said later when she was able to
catch her breath, "I don't know if I can stand any
more of this in one night."

He laughed. "You asked for it and you are in no

position to bargain. I've got you just where I want you, Marilyn. And I'm not about to let you go."

But suddenly, someone at the front door began to hammer loudly.

"Damn!" Marilyn cried. "Who could it be at this hour! I haven't had a visitor since the day after the funeral."

"Whoever it is, let's ignore him," Clint decided. "If we do maybe he'll go away."

But he was wrong. "Gunsmith!" Sheriff Fox bellowed, "I know that you're in there 'cause I see your muddy boot tracks! Open up, there's something important I have to tell you."

Marilyn sighed beneath him. "I suppose you had better do as he asks before he creates such a stir the whole neighborhood will be peeking out their windows and wondering what we are up to."

"Whatever they suspect, it will probably be true," Clint said, as he rolled off and pulled her late husband's clean dry trousers on.

"Gunsmith, dammit, this is important!"

"I'm coming!" he yelled, shrugging into William Tippett's smoking jacket and hurrying to the door. "Keep your voice down, you fool!"

The sheriff was standing on the porch and the rain was still falling. He looked bedraggled and thoroughly miserable but Clint did not invite him inside.

"What is so important it couldn't wait until morning?" he demanded.

"Dr. Evans treated little Maggie Perdue for a gunshot to the thigh. Lola and Rosie brought her in last night just after dark."

"Why didn't he tell us sooner!"

"Because they wrote a note saying he had an emergency call twenty-five miles out of town and would not be back until late this evening. When he failed to return, his family started searching for him.''

"And?"

"They found Dr. Evans with a very nasty gash over his ear where Lola Perdue had pistol-whipped him just before she tied him up and locked the poor man in a coat closet. He'd been there for almost twenty hours!''

Clint shook his head. "Was he able to give you any idea of the direction they were heading?''

"Not a clue,'' the sheriff answered in a downcast voice.

"What about Maggie Perdue? How bad was the bullet wound in her leg?''

"Not all that bad. It bled a good deal and would have become infected had it not been treated. But the doctor said that, while painful, it should not cause the girl any more trouble.''

Clint frowned. "I should think it would make riding a horse very painful.''

"Probably. But you know that Lola won't let her stop and heal the wound. They're on the run.''

"And we still haven't any idea which direction.''

"That's right,'' the sheriff said. "So I guess all we got is those telegrams you sent out late this afternoon. I thought you might want to check the telegraph office tonight.''

Clint looked out at the sleeting rain. He glanced back over his shoulder at the warm fireplace light that flowed like honey out into the hallway and parlor.

"I don't think so,'' he said. "I'll check on them tomorrow morning. Too late and miserable out to travel until then anyway.''

The sheriff shook his head with disgust. "Some lawman,'' he growled but added with a rueful grin, "still, with a woman like Marilyn Tippett waiting in bed, I'd think you were goddamn crazy if you left in the next week!''

Clint chuckled. "Good night, Sheriff," he said as he closed the door and bolted the lock.

"Lucky son of a bitch," he heard Fox mutter as he tromped off through the sloppy sea of churned mud.

SEVENTEEN

On his way out of Ft. Worth five days later, Clint stopped at Marilyn Tippett's picket gate and tied his horse. The rain had stopped falling and he felt good and rested. Sure, there was a hell of a lot of water and mud, but once Clint left town, he knew that he would find the prairie dry and the traveling easier.

Marilyn came out to meet him on the porch. "Can't you come into my parlor and say good-bye a little more . . . personally?" she asked.

"We said our good mornings in bed and that was about as personal as it gets between a man and a woman."

Marilyn shrugged her shoulders. She was trying to keep it light between them even though the news of his leaving had come as a shock and disappointment. "I didn't think you'd hear any news about the Perdue gang so quickly."

She opened her purse and took out a sheaf of bills. "This is a thousand dollars for you."

"I don't need it," he protested.

"Of course you do. Clint, forgive me but I took the foul liberty of checking your wallet a couple of days ago. You were down to eight dollars. Surely you can't begin this hunt broke."

Clint frowned. "I've hunted men broke before and it never seemed to have made much of a difference as to whether or not I caught them."

"Please take the money. You may need it to buy information. Lola is so devious, she will do anything to stop you once she learns you are on her trail. I want you to have the best possible chance of catching her and the others and bringing them to trial."

He took the money. She was rich and he was poor. And she really wanted him to have it. "No strings?"

"None whatsoever. The money is yours to spend as you see fit. Gamble it away, you can even use it to buy pleasure."

"Uh-uh," he told her. "I've never spent a cent buying a woman's favors. If something isn't given freely, it isn't worth taking."

"That money is given very freely, Clint. You've taught me what it feels like to be loved and a woman again. I don't expect you to marry me or anything. I just want you to be as happy as you have made me this past week."

He blushed a little with embarrassment and seeing it, she fell silent.

"The neighbors are watching," Clint said. "There will be a lot of gossip. Might be hard on you, Marilyn."

"To the devil with my nosy neighbors. When you're poor or in need, things like public opinion count. But I'm rich and, thanks to the artistry of your lovemaking, I don't need their approval. I can stand on my own now and, Gunsmith, it will take quite a man to match you. Quite a man."

She threw her arms around his neck and her slender body melted to his own. "Let's give them a send-off to really talk about!"

Clint kissed her hard and long. Her mouth opened and his tongue moved inside her and it took all the willpower he had not to scoop her up into his arms and carry her back into the house for another session of lovemaking.

But instead, he took the money and stuffed it into his pocket. A telegraph from Big Spring told him that Lola, Maggie and Rosie had been through town and had won a big horse race. Said they had probably pocketed over two thousand dollars between them and were last heading in the direction of El Paso where it was rumored that some very fast horses could be found to race.

Clint rode out of Ft. Worth passing the sheriff's office. Fox and several people waved, but a lot of them still felt anger about the entire Perdue affair and smarted over the fact that the Gunsmith alone had not been fooled by that dramatic testimony.

To the devil with them too, he thought, remembering Marilyn Tippett's words regarding her gossipy neighbors. All that counted now was finding Lola Perdue, Maggie and poor Rosie. He just hoped he was not too late.

Clint arrived in Big Spring, Texas five days later, tired, but confident that he was on the right trail. He had stopped along the way at a little trading post on the Colorado River and learned that the three outlaw women had passed through nearly a week earlier. They had been seen riding three common saddle horses and leading the tall, flashy thoroughbred, Crimson Victory. Lola and Rosie were so damned good looking they were easily remembered and that racing stallion was sure not your everyday cowpony.

At Big Spring, Clint went right to the sheriff's office and shook the massive hand of a man named T.B. Gutmeyer. The sheriff was a huge, florid-faced German who looked more like St. Nicholas than a real lawman.

"Yeah sure, you bet I remember them," Gutmeyer said, with a sad shake of his head after Clint had given his famous name. "They cleaned out the town at that horse race. Won maybe five thousand dollars. Terrible around here. Then we had a bank robbery two days later. I tell you, this town is in a terrible fix!"

"You had a bank robbery?"

"That's what I said."

"Any suspects?"

"Not a one. Somehow, they broke into the bank at night and opened the safe. Took everything. About six thousand dollars."

"Inside job?"

"I don't think so."

"Someone had to give them the vault's combination."

The lawman shrugged. He was slope-shouldered in the way of most really powerful men. "I questioned everyone."

"How about the banker himself?"

"Donald James?" The lawman sat up straight in his chair. "Now, why would he want to steal from his own bank?"

Clint shook his head. He imagined the big German was a hell of a force to stop drunken barroom brawls before they started just by sheer size and physical intimidation, but the man was certainly lacking imagination.

"Let's put it this way," Clint said. "Let's say that you or a very close friend or relative bet on a favorite horse against an outsider's horse. Bet more money than you had any right to bet, what would you do if you had a very, very friendly banker?''

"I would ask him to loan me the money to cover the bet," the German said with a frown.

"Which," Clint said, "he might just do—unless he had also bet too heavily, or, all his depositors had bet too heavily and withdrawn their cash deposits leaving the bank nearly insolvent. In that case, you might expect there would be an almost irresistable temptation to fake a bank theft and then throw up your hands and squall like you had been robbed.''

"I can't believe that is possible. But I have to tell you this. The horse that lost belonged to Mr. James.''

Clint beamed. "In that case, I suggest you invite the man over right this minute so we can ask him a few pointed questions.''

"Like what?''

"I don't know," Clint admitted. "Let's just play it by ear and see what happens.''

The sheriff nodded and rose from his seat. "I could lose my job for this in the upcoming election," he said worriedly. "I'll probably lose it anyway. I have a wife and a baby on the way. This is a nice, peaceful town and I want to keep this job.''

"Then look at this as an opportunity. If we get a signed confession of guilt, you'll be reelected for the next thirty years.''

Gutmeyer liked that possibility. "I'll do it," he said simply. "You're sure you are the famous Gunsmith?''

"I am sure.''

"All right, I'll go and get him then.''

Clint took the sheriff's seat and put his feet up on the scarred desk. For some reason, he liked T. B.

Gutmeyer. The man should have been a blacksmith
or a wheelright but he was doing the best he could
given his abilities. Besides, Clint hated sneaky criminals like he suspected the banker might well be.
They were men who did not have the courage to
openly go after what they wanted. Instead, they
wormed their way into the public trust and then
misused that trust to fill their own pockets. Catching
one crook like Donald James was worth catching a
half-dozen minor thugs and thieves, or arresting an
entire jail full of drunks and hell raisers on a Saturday night.

Ten minutes later, they returned.

"What the hell is going on here!" a man in a black
suit, white shirt and tie demanded assertively. "Who
the hell is this, Gutmeyer!"

"His name is the Gunsmith."

"Odd name. Why the hell is he sitting behind your
desk! Gutmeyer, I told you we are not giving you
even one stinking deputy. Besides, after the upcoming election, you'll be out on your dumb ass and
looking for a job cleaning stalls or something."

Gutmeyer stiffened and his pale cheeks grew pink
with humiliation. He looked to Clint and nodded
hopefully. It was now quite obvious why the sheriff
of Big Spring was playing along with Clint's game.

"Mr. James, I have a question or two I need to ask
you about a woman named Lola Perdue and her
friends."

"Why should I know anything about them!" He
glared defiantly. "Or for that matter, why should I
even answer your question!"

Clint did not bat an eye. He wasn't going to get
anywhere making mild threats with this man. The
only way to tell if Donald James was a crook or not
was by hitting the pompous banker right between the

eyes with a hammer blow and then letting the chips fall where they may.

"You'll answer all my questions because you lost a great deal of money betting on your own horse and then robbed your own bank to cover the losses."

"What!"

"Sure," Clint said, with a relaxed smile. "I've just come from El Paso where we have arrested Lola Perdue and her gang. She was carrying a large amount of money and admitted that you helped her rob this bank. I'm here to arrest and take you to trial. A signed confession before the face-to-face courtroom hearing will go a long way toward reducing your prison sentence."

The banker's face drained itself of blood until it was the color of slate marble. "Lola is lying!" he screeched brokenly.

Clint shrugged and climbed to his feet and made as if to draw his six-gun. "Fine. Let's go to El Paso and get you a twenty year prison sentence, Mr. James."

The man faltered back a step. "Wait," he breathed, reaching for a monogrammed handkerchief and mopping his brow as sweat burst across his forehead. "How . . . how much of a reduction would I get if I sign your confession and give back what money I have left?"

Gutmeyer looked so stunned by this new and sudden line of questioning that his mouth fell open and when he tried to speak, Clint shut him off. "Probably a year or two. Maybe you'll even get a jail sentence instead of being forced to go to the big federal prison which is—for a man of your delicate nature— the land of no-return."

"I see," James choked. "Get me a paper and quill."

"Sheriff?"

Gutmeyer started as if awakening from a dream.

He leaped for a paper and quill and then watched open-mouthed as Donald James wrote a full confession which Clint witnessed.

"Will you still need to take me to El Paso?" James asked in a trembling voice.

"First you show Sheriff Gutmeyer where you hid the bank money. Afterward, we can talk about the details."

The banker nodded dumbly. He was too shocked to think straight. Later, when he realized he had been tricked, he would no doubt hire the town's best attorney and deny everything. But by then his signed confession along with the money would be too great a case to fight against.

No question about it, Donald James was going to prison.

"I'll . . . I'll be back in a few minutes," Gutmeyer said. "With the money."

Clint nodded. "Take your time. Grab a friend to go along with you just in case, and then have him witness this confession as well. If James tries to escape, shoot to kill!"

Clint looked deep into the banker's eyes. "I almost hope you do try to escape."

"Oh, God! I swear I won't!"

"Take him away, Sheriff."

Gutmeyer grabbed the man by the arm and almost threw him at the door. "Thank you, Gunsmith," he said, grateful blue eyes brimming with admiration. "I shall never forget this."

Clint winked. "Not as long as you are this town's sheriff you won't."

Clint let them leave. He walked out to the hitching rail and untied Duke. He saw Gutmeyer hail a friendly witness and that was the final link to an airtight case of grand theft.

The Gunsmith climbed on his horse and rode

toward El Paso. This Donald James thing had not ac-
complished anything toward helping him catch Lola
Perdue. But it had not taken much time and, besides,
Gutmeyer was a good, honest man who tried hard.
Maybe he'd get a little sharper during his next thirty
years in office.

EIGHTEEN

Rosie could feel Crimson Victory tense as Maggie Perdue led her race horse toward the starting line. Behind her, half the citizens of El Paso stood waiting under the clear, hot sun. Ahead of her a mile and a quarter down this hard, dirt road waited the other half.

With the exception of the Gunsmith's black gelding, the dapple-gray stallion which waited at the finish line was the most magnificent horse Rosie had ever seen.

The animal was even taller than Crimson Victory and more powerful looking. It had been raced forty-six times and never been beaten, tied, or even seriously challenged. Rosie looked ahead down the race-course and thought very seriously about just starting out and then veering northwest and letting her horse run and run.

But there really was no place to run. She was an outlaw and to go it alone meant certain death. They could come into a town and stay one day or two to

109

make a quick killing on a horse race, but then they had to move on before word of their presence got back to Ft. Worth. Tonight, they were going to slip across the border into Mexico and hide out for a few days, and then loop back up into New Mexico heading for that Nevada mustanging ranch. A ranch that had, for Rosie, become her sole reason for existing. She could not imagine going through life on the run, constantly moving from one town and horse race to the next until either she or Crimson Victory gave out or lost the will to live. Some people believed in heaven; Rosie's heaven was a Nevada horse ranch somewhere so far from civilization that she would never have to worry about her past.

"Rosie," Maggie Perdue whispered, her voice barely audible over the roaring and shouting of the crowd, "We got four to one odds. If we win, we'll make eight thousand dollars."

"But I don't think we can win," Rosie said, eyeing their magnificent opponent.

"Yes we will."

Rosie glanced down at the thin, colorless woman. It always amazed her to realize that Maggie and Lola were real sisters. The two could not have been more unalike. Maggie was plain, frail, shy and totally submissive to her older sister. Lola was a real looker and completely ruthless with anyone who dared to cross her path. Lola was a killer, Maggie was a frightened mouse of a woman barely capable of holding a six-gun, much less using it. In Big Spring, even though the bank robbery had been set up by Mr. James, Maggie had been so nervous that she had been violently ill.

Rosie shook her head with pity for the woman. She herself might escape on this big red stallion, but that would not help Maggie; the poor girl needed help before she was shot to death trying to help her sister rob some goddamn bank.

They neared the starting line. The jockey on the gray stallion was an old veteran like Bennie only he was ruggedly handsome despite his lack of stature. They had already met and Rosie recalled that his name was Earl. Earl had ridden El Paso's thorough-bred champion in every one of those forty-six victories.

"You ready?" the jockey asked her with a quick, confident grin as he rode in much too close.

"Get back!" Rosie cried, knowing that two hot-blooded stallions would fight and wondering how a veteran rider like Earl could be so careless.

Her warning came too late as Crimson Victory squalled at his rival and lashed out with a foreleg. The handsome gray took the blow on its shoulder and before it could retaliate, men jumped between the two horses, grabbed their bits and pulled them away from each other.

Rosie was trembling. People got killed trying to step between two stallions. The crowd was shouting and pushing to get a look at the gray whose name was Silver Shot.

"Is he all right!" she cried.

The jockey nodded grimly. "He's fine. Dammit, let's get this over with!"

Rosie heard men arguing fiercely and then Earl whipped the stallion forward and it lunged to the starting line and began to whirl around and around. "Let's go!" Earl shouted. "Fire that goddamn gun before these two really get to fighting!"

The starter raised his pistol. Rosie glanced at Maggie and then at the gray which had a bloodied shoulder. This just was not right!

The gun exploded and Crimson Victory was ready

even if she was not. The red stallion hurled itself forward and then the crowd was screaming and the race
was on. Silver Shot was half-turned and left in her
dust.

But at the half mile marker, Silver Shot was able to
make up his poor start and overtake Rosie.

Now, as they swept past the three-quarter mile
marker, they were racing stride for matched stride, a
swirling blur of light and dark legs which devoured
the distance. Rosie was up in her stirrups, body forward over the withers so that her weight was perfectly
distributed. She sensed and heard rather than actually saw the crowd as they swept past hundreds of
screaming Texans.

And then, even though Crimson Victory was flying, the dapple gray stallion began to inch ahead.
Just a little, then a nose, then a full head and as they
neared the mile marker, the stallion was half a length
ahead.

Crimson Victory was game and not about to quit.
He ran with his ears back and his heart on the line.
Rosie could feel his body straining, hear his tortured
breath tearing in and out of his distended nostrils.
Her gallant horse ran with everything he had but he
was outmatched. But then suddenly, as they passed
the mile marker, the dapple seemed to lose its tremendous, flowing stride. It faltered, gathered itself
and faltered again as Rosie and her horse swept past.

The crowd was going insane! Rosie felt the dapple
coming back at her but it was too late. She and her
horse were sailing across the finish line a full length
ahead.

She had a difficult time stopping Crimson Victory
and so did Earl. Rosie finally managed to get her
horse under control and, as she turned him back
toward the crowd which was roaring in anger, she ex-

pected to see the beautiful dapple stallion pull up
lame. But it did not.

"What happened back there!" she cried.

The handsome jockey avoided her eyes. He
shrugged and let the handlers grab Silver Shot. Then
he leapt from his saddle and was quickly swallowed
up by a furious crowd that had bet heavily on its local
favorite.

Rosie shook her head in momentary bewilderment.
Suddenly, she understood. The race had been fixed
so that she would win! There had never been a question of the outcome and that meant that the owner
and Earl had bet against their own horse. And that
moment before the race when Crimson Victory
struck Silver Shot, that had all been a calculated
gamble. A gamble that the gray would not sustain
any serious injury, but that the crowd would assume
the attack was the reason for their favorite's upset
loss. In the minds of the citizens of El Paso, the
defeat of their favorite would appear to be a fluke,
the result of an injury. They would believe Silver
Shot had not really been fairly defeated.

"Hell of a ride," Lola said, smiling broadly. "You
sure earned champagne and steak tonight."

But Rosie didn't answer. When she looked out at
the crowd and thought about all the bettors who had
been swindled out of their money, she felt rotten inside.

"I think we had better get out of this town and into
Mexico," she said, "before this crowd realizes what
really happened."

Lola looked at the sea of bitter, angry faces. For
once, she actually looked unnerved. "I think you're
right," she said. "We'll collect our bets and move
out fast."

"No banks."

Lola laughed only it wasn't a pleasant sound. "After this haul, we don't need any of that this time. Come on, let's see if we can find a fast Mexican horse to beat south of the border."

"What about Nevada?" Rosie demanded.

"We're going, honey. Just don't push me."

Rosie bit back her angry reply. She reined Crimson Victory sharply and was immediately sorry. "It's not your fault," she said, as she patted the stallion's sweaty neck. "You're the only one among us who is honest."

NINETEEN

When Clint galloped into El Paso, the folks were still talking about the horse race and how Silver Shot should not have been run after being injured by Crimson Victory. The whole town was furious and there were a lot of people who had lost their entire savings on that race.

Clint went to see the sheriff, a man named Reece Coddington and after the introductions, Clint came right to the point. "Those Perdue sisters are wanted for bank robbery, horse thievery and a list as long as your arm."

"Is that a fact?" The sheriff was in his early thirties, a hatchet-faced man with a dirty, wrinkled shirt and custom-made boots that must have cost fifty dollars. Clint had disliked the lawman at first sight. You could forgive a fella for being poor, but not for being slovenly.

"It is," Clint said.

"Well, how about that! Any reward?"

Clint pulled out a reward poster that he had man-

aged to pry out of another sheriff. Lola Perdue was
dark-haired in the picture, but the overall
resemblance was unmistakable.

"She's gone and changed her hair color," the
sheriff grunted. "What about the scrawny one and
the one with the big tits?"

Clint checked the urge to reach out and slap this
man out of his chair. "Maggie Perdue is also wanted
for the same crimes and has a reward on her head for
capture."

"And big tits?"

"No reward," Clint said tightly, "at least there
isn't yet."

"She's part of the gang, ain't she?"

"She's different," Clint said.

"I'll say. You should have seen her on top of that
big red stallion. I swear the menfolk in this town forgot the horse, they were so damned busy getting an
eyeful of the rider."

He studied Clint with suspicion. "This is my ter-
ritory, hereabouts. I guess I'll thank you to let me
and my deputies apprehend these little gals. We don't
need any of your help."

Clint saw him start to put Lola's reward poster in
his drawer. The Gunsmith clamped his hand down on
the sheriff's. "That's mine," he said. "I'll be having
it back."

The sheriff was not happy. His eyes blazed with
anger but when Clint stood up across from his desk,
the sheriff seemed to understand that he was pushing
hard trouble.

"All right, Gunsmith," he growled. "You keep
the poster. We don't need it anyway. And as for
those three, I'll see that they are brought to justice."

"Where did they go?" Clint demanded.

The sheriff laughed coldly. "Do you actually think

I'm so dumb that I'm going to let you grab them for the reward?"

"I want Rosalie," Clint said. "The other two are the ones that there's a reward on their heads."

"What you want her for besides the obvious reasons? She your woman?"

Clint decided it would be useless to try to explain that Rosie didn't deserve the same fate as Lola, or even Maggie would receive. She was different, at least she used to be different.

"Yeah," he said. "And if you call her 'big tits' again, I'm going to slam your teeth through your big mouth."

"Get outa here," the sheriff hissed. "If she's a part of the gang, she has a reward on her head too."

Clint folded the reward poster and slipped it into his pocket. "You're going to mess things up, aren't you, Sheriff?"

"I'm going to get a whole lot richer is what I'm going to do," the man snapped. "Now get the hell out of El Paso."

"I'll go when I'm damn good and ready," Clint told the man. "And I don't take to being pushed so keep your distance from me."

Coddington stood up and his face got ugly. "I hear of you in any trouble at all, we'll run you out of this town on a rail."

"You can try," Clint said, "but my advice would be to tell me which way those three women rode out and let me go when I damn well feel like it."

There was nothing more that Clint could say so he headed for the street. Duke was worn-out and so was he. Clint opted for a livery and a hotel room. He especially liked the looks of the one across the street that overlooked the sheriff's office. Unless he missed his bet, Coddington and at least one of his deputies

would be hitting the outlaw trail just as soon as they
thought the Gunsmith's back was turned.

Sheriff Coddington waited until midnight and then
he took a deputy with him to Mexico. Clint had Duke
saddled again and ready. The sheriff rode one mile to
the Rio Grande and then splashed into the moonlit
water that lifted before his horse's hooves like liquid
gold. At this time of year, the river was little more
than a muddy stream. Clint waited until the sheriff
and his friend were across the river and then he urged
Duke forward. The moment he entered Juárez the
Gunsmith was swallowed up by the smells and
sounds of the big Mexican town.

Clint rode cautiously for the simple reason that
there were Mexican *banditos* and gunmen who would
kill for his horse, saddle and six-gun. Clint had heard
of it happening too many times in the past. A cowboy, probably drunk and in a part of town where he
would ordinarily know better than to be at night,
would suddenly see a shadow of movement and then,
in the last terrified moment of his life, see the fatal
flash of muzzle fire. His body would fall and before
his blood jelled, he would be stripped clean and
rolled into a ditch or the brush. In the morning,
people might see his naked corpse but no one would
look twice or dare to ask questions. Not in a border
town like Juárez where life was too plentiful and
very, very cheap.

He had lost the sheriff and his friend, but Clint
was not overly concerned by this. He circled the main
part of town to arrive at the southern exit road. He
dismounted and waited two full hours. Satisfied that
the sheriff was not coming through on his way deeper
into Mexico, the Gunsmith concluded that Rosie and
the Perdue women were hiding somewhere in the
teaming squalor of Juárez.

I will find them tomorrow, he thought. They will not be expecting me here and this place is not so big that three white women and their horses can remain hidden for very long.

With that decision made, the Gunsmith rode out into the desert a couple more miles. He found a hidden place among the rocks and cacti and untied his bedroll. It was a dry camp but he did not mind and the night was growing short.

Clint flopped down on his blanket and stared up at a full moon so bright it almost obliterated the stars from their heavens. He thought about Rosie and about the other pair she rode with. He was not sure what he would do when he caught them. Finding them was one thing, getting them out of Mexico could be yet another.

Tomorrow was going to be an interesting day.

TWENTY

Lola Perdue was entertaining one of the richest men in El Paso, a man who had the dubious reputation of having ruslted more cattle than any man in West Texas. Owner of thoroughbred race horses and collector of fast women, Bart Raymond was a scoundrel and a con man.

Lola found him too cocky, though she had to admit that the stories she had heard about him were fantastic. He was said to be an extraordinary lover and a knife fighter. A man who proclaimed himself without equal in both those areas, even when down here among the lusty banditos of Juárez. The knife fighter part was no doubt true for Raymond possessed at least two knife scars that she could see and it was said that his long, hard body carried a half dozen more. As for his other talent, the *senoritas* swore this as also true.

They were sitting in a Juárez *cantina* where you did not enter except by consent of men who controlled by power. The room was crowded, a dancing girl entertained the crowd and a six-piece band—all trumpets and guitars—played much too loudly.

Raymond had to almost shout to be heard. "If we do this correctly," he said, slipping his arm around Lola's slender waist and pulling her closer as he squinted through blue cigar smoke at the dancing senorita's long, flashing legs, "we can each make at least twenty thousand dollars!"

Lola allowed him to fondle her a little before she pulled away with an encouraging smile meant to prolong his anticipation. She had a strong appetite for strong men but she had learned that it was better to discuss business before allowing herself to become lost in carnal pleasure.

"Let's talk about that first," she said. "Are you sure that we can do that well?"

"Of course. Maybe even better." Raymond leaned forward, his hand sliding seductively to where her legs met. "Listen to me my dear Lola. After that first race, everybody believes my horse was lamed by yours. They want revenge. They saw Silver Shot come back and pass your stallion but then suddenly go off stride. They are sure it was due to the injury your horse gave mine at the starting line. Now, they'll bet everything that my healthy animal can outrun yours."

"But Rosie says that he really can. She says that Crimson Victory is not Silver Shot's equal."

"I know that. So does everyone in El Paso. So when they have a rematch, they'll all bet on my horse again."

"And . . . and he will lose again?"

Raymond grinned. "Exactly. And we will get far better odds than before. We bet everything on your animal and walk away with the town's money and it's perfectly legal!"

"Those people in El Paso will never let us get out of there alive."

Raymond nodded, the smile dying on his lips. "That's right. They'll pay off and then extract nothing less than flesh and blood."

"Whose?"

"Guess," Raymond said, taking a sip of his tequila.

"Not me or Maggie."

"Of course not."

"Rosie?"

"Who else? Her and the horse. As soon as we have collected our fortune, I'll have someone shout that the race was fixed. That he saw Rosie drug our horse. And Silver Shot will be drugged enough so that he can't possibly win."

Lola thought it over carefully. She weighed every angle and found nothing lacking. "They'll lynch Rosie."

"Of course they will. I'll tell the sheriff to just stay the hell away until she's dead. There is something else you should be aware of, my dear. They will also kill your own race horse."

"Why!"

Raymond shrugged as if the matter were of no importance at all. "I don't know. It's just the way they will feel. Silver Shot is the champion of El Paso. They'll believe he was twice cheated by a lesser horse and they'll kill that animal as sure as we are going to find a bed within the next hour."

Lola Perdue took a big drink. "All right," she said. "I don't mind the girl getting lynched. She's a soft-bellied bitch who would turn us in sooner or later. The only thing that has kept her in this game so far is the threat of prison and the promise of a mustang ranch."

Lola giggled. "Can you imagine the fool believing

someone like me would live on a goddamn mustang ranch!''

Raymond moved his hand under her dress and began to explore. "She must indeed be a fool," he said a little thickly. "But it is a pity to see such a good looking woman die young."

Lola shifted in her chair so that he could explore her even better. "Yeah," she said, her voice starting to go hoarse with passion, "but ain't it a damn crying shame about my horse."

They were just about to leave the table and head for a room when Sheriff Reece Coddington appeared.

"Boss," he said, tipping his hat to Lola who glared at him for interrupting their play. "We got big trouble."

Bart Raymond pulled his hand out from between Lola's parted legs. He was all business now. "Let's hear it."

"It's the Gunsmith. He's in town asking about Miss Perdue and the other two. I told him to leave El Paso but he won't scare. He's on their trail and he means to stick."

Lola swore. "There goes our big killing at the races," she said. "If he's in town, the race will never take place."

"Why didn't you tell me such a man was on your trail?"

"Because I didn't know!" Lola hissed angrily. "The last I saw of him, he was in Ft Worth."

Reece Coddington chimed in. "He says that Rosie is his woman. He meant it too."

Raymond leaned back and lit a cigar. Lola was forgotten for the moment. "We'll have to find him and kill him before race time," he said. "It should not be difficult."

"Killing the Gunsmith not difficult!" Sheriff Coddington shook his head in disbelief. "I wouldn't face him backed by the three fastest gunmen in El Paso."

"That's because he'd kill you first. But the second, third or fourth man would down him," Raymond said. "Besides, I have no intention of sending gunfighters to kill an even better gunfighter."

"Then how?"

Raymond reached down into his boot top and pulled out a Bowie knife. It was a sinister looking weapon, with a foot-long blade that could stab like a dagger, slice like a razor and chop like a sword. It weighed exactly one pound and had a pearl and silver handle just like the one that Jim Bowie had used at the Alamo.

"You're going to stick the Gunsmith?" Lola asked sharply.

"Of course not. Unless the knife fighters I hire to find and kill him fail. In that case, I would consider it a great pleasure to do the job myself just before the race begins."

Lola nodded with admiration. "You're as brave and smart as I heard you were."

He grinned. Returned the Bowie knife to his boot top and then slipped his hand back between her legs. "And what else have you heard, lovely woman?"

Lola giggled. "Guess?"

He finished his tequila with a toss of the glass and rose, his own passion making him anxious. "Sheriff," he said, "go back to El Paso and spread the word that there will be a second horse race next Sunday. This time, a race that will prove who is the real champion."

"But everybody will bet on Silver Shot again, so—"

"So we bet on Miss Perdue's gallant red stallion a second time, eh?"

The sheriff blinked. "But they'll riot in the streets and howl for blood!"

"We know," Lola said, "but so long as they get it and it's not our own, does it matter?"

Sheriff Reece Coddington shook his head and walked away quickly.

TWENTY-ONE

Clint awoke two hours after sunrise with the feeling that something was definitely wrong. He opened his eyes and reached for his gun but the familiar cocking of three rifles made him freeze.

"*Senor*, you slept well, *si*?"

Clint rolled over and saw three gaily dressed Mexican bandits standing with their weapons aimed at his chest. Granted, they were old weapons but Clint had no doubt that any of them could kill him.

The leader of the three colorful outlaws was a fat man about Clint's age who stood less than five and a half feet tall but who must have weighed almost three hundred pounds. He had an immense girth and wore three bandoliers of bullets around his enormous chest and shoulders. Clint could also see two pistols and two big knives sticking out from behind his cartridge belt.

"Juan," the fat bandit said, "hees gun."

Juan jumped forward, but he was careful and did not make the mistake of passing in between Clint and

his friends and thus providing the Gunsmith with a
moment to draw and fire.

"Pistol, *senor!*"

Like his leader, Juan spoke pretty decent English
and Clint had the suspicion that these three operated
on both sides of the border. Clint momentarily considered attempting a border switch on the man but
that vanished when the other two stepped forward
and poked their rifle barrels into his face. He handed
over his gun.

"Mind if I get up now?"

They motioned for him to stand. The fat one
studied him, then looked down at Clint's boots. He
snatched them up and tried them on. They were too
small and he cursed. Juan tried them on and they
were too large. But the third bandit grinned happily
and walked around showing how well the Gunsmith's
custom-made boots fit. Clint knew he had lost his
boots.

"You have nice horse, *si, gringo*?"

Clint stiffened. "Yes," he said. "But a little
loco."

"Loco?" The fat Mexican laughed. He did not
believe it for a minute. "Jose, you saddle hees horse
for me."

Jose nodded and went to saddle Duke while the
other two held their rifles on Clint. The Gunsmith
smiled grimly. Duke was a one man horse.

Oh, sure, Rosie had ridden him during the race in
Ft. Worth, but the big gelding had gotten accus-
tomed to her slowly and seemed to understand that
she was Clint's friend. This was entirely another matter. Jose wore the typical big Spanish rowels on his
spurs, which he had attached to Clint's boots and
Duke would not tolerate that for a moment.

Duke waited nervously as he was bridled and saddled. He kep glancing at the Gunsmith as if to ask him what in the hell was this man up to. And then, Jose sprang into the saddle and the rawhide whip in his hand slashed Duke across the rump.

The black exploded into the sky. He came down stiff legged and despite everything that Jose could do to keep his head up, Duke took the bit between his teeth, lowered his head between his forelegs and slung the Mexican a good thirty feet into a pile of cacti.

"Eiiiiieh!" Jose screamed.

The fat bandit cursed in Spanish and then sent Juan to help his friend. When they finally got Jose straightened out, Clint stood back and listened to them jabber away in Spanish. The Gunsmith was not the least fluent himself, but he did get the gist of the conversation and it revolved around the fact that Jose was by far the best rider and yet he was dead set against climbing on Duke's back again. At least not today and not out on an open range littered with cactus plants.

The fat leader's name was Manuel and he was incensed at the way things had gone. At first, he wanted to shoot Duke, but knew that Clint would attack him bare-handed before allowing that to happen.

"Let me get him," Clint offered. "He is just a horse. You have my boots, my gun. Why not allow me my life and my horse? What harm?"

They argued about that and decided that the horse was too good to let go so easily. They would take it to a *vaquero* named Escobar down in Mexico who would break the animal and then it would sell for much money north of the border.

As they talked, Clint struggled to find some way to gain the upper hand. He knew that these men would not show him mercy. They were ruthless bandits who probably took and sold women and children as well as animals.

It was decided that Jose should rope Duke and the horse would be led south to the vaquero's *rancho*. Clint watched as Jose moved stiffly to his own horse and then mounted very gingerly. He shook out his fifty foot leather *rieta* and rode toward Duke. The gelding knew what was coming and he moved off.

Suddenly, Jose drove his spurs into his horse and the animal shot forward. The *rieta* whirred and then jumped out of the Mexican's hand as if it were alive. It reached out and grabbed Duke around the throat like a fist but before Jose could get a good dally on his saddlehorn, Duke hit the end of the *rieta* and it was torn from Jose's fist as Duke raced south with his tail high in the air.

The Mexican screamed in fury and the palm of his hand was burned and torn deeply by the rieta. At that moment, Clint jumped for the rifle in Juan's fist. He got his hands on it and managed to slam the stock upward into the bandit's jaw. Juan staggered but he held on and that was the difference as the huge Manuel raised his own rifle overhead. Clint saw the weapon flash in the sun and he tried to twist out of the way but only partly succeeded. With a blinding flash behind his eyes, the rifle crashed against his skull and he went spiraling into a sea of utter darkness.

TWENTY-TWO

There are times in everyone's life when fate seems to twist back and forth like a steep mountain road going nowhere except straight up or straight down. All the Gunsmith's luck had been bad since he had crossed into Mexico but now, as he gazed up into the troubled face of a senorita, he thought he was looking into the eyes of an angel in heaven.

He was in a cool, shadowed room, but he could see sunlight burning through cracks in the rock walls. The young woman was mopping his face with water and there was sorrow in her eyes. Clint saw a heavy wooden crucifix behind her and then he heard a hushed voice in Spanish.

The young woman turned and Clint saw a very old man dressed in a white peon's outfit. The man had silver hair and a long white mustache. His face was deeply lined and in his hands he carried a hoe.

Clint understood now. He had been found by someone who believed in mercy and kindness and brought to this little house. He was not in heaven at all.

Clint tried to sit up but the pain in his head made
that impossible for the moment. He groaned and the
woman bit her lip.

"You are beautiful," he told her, "and, to me,
you are still an angel."

She smiled as the worry fled her expression. Clint
knew she did not understand a word he had spoken.

"Help me sit up," he said, reaching for her shoulder.

The old man jumped forward and raised his hoe to
strike. The girl cried out and begged for Clint's life.
Clint smiled and thought that this would be one hell
of an ignoble way for a gunfighter to die.

The girl prevailed and Clint realized he had been
holding his breath. The old farmer lowered his hoe
and walked outside.

"Whew!" Clint said, rolling his eyes in pretended
fear.

The girl understood and her sudden burst of laughter filled the room. She got up and went to bring
him tortillas and goat's milk which he enjoyed
thoroughly.

Clint touched his head and found that she had
bound his scalp with rags. He gently pulled them off
despite her protests and then he sat up. A moment
later he pushed himself to his feet.

The girl tried to get him to lie back on the bed but
Clint knew he could not wait another moment. Down
south, Duke would be facing a man named Escobar
who would use all his skills to break the gelding's
spirit so that it could be ridden.

Clint staggered to the door of the rock hut and
looked outside. All he saw was the old man hoeing a
small, rocky patch of earth. There was a stick and
brush corral and one skinny burro.

"*Senor!*" Clint called.

The girl's father stopped beating at the rocky dirt

and stunted weeds. He straightened up and mopped his brow. Clint stepped out into the bright sunlight and his vision momentarily spun. He lurched sideways at the door and the girl caught him and tried to drag him back into the rock hut. But the Gunsmith shook his aching head. *"Senor, por favor!"* he cried.

The old man came forward. Somehow, Clint had to make him understand that he needed to borrow the burro and a weapon. A gun if possible, but if not, even an axe.

"Senor," Clint began, searching for the words to tell his sad tale. He sat down before the doorway and used his hands and a stick to draw pictures in the soft, powdery dirt.

An hour later, he was riding the burro south. There was a thick wooden staff a yard long in one of his fists and old leather sandals protected the soles of his feet. He wore a *serape* and because the bandits had stolen his Stetson, he also wore a *sombrero* which was pulled down over his broken head right to the eyebrows.

To anyone passing, he looked to be just another starving peon. But he was the Gunsmith, and there were men down south who were going to pay.

Clint found his campsite immediately and then followed Duke's trail. It was easy. The three bandits believed they had no reason to hide.

As he rode, the Gunsmith's sandaled feet almost dragged along the desert floor but the valiant little burro walked steadily, mile after blistering mile. The day grew very hot and when the burro finally began to stagger and weaken, the Gunsmith climbed off it and stretched out to nap in the shade of a giant cactus. He awoke late in the afternoon feeling rested and they continued on.

The Gunsmith came upon the vaquero's ranch just before sunset. Clint might never even have seen it except that he saw a cloud of dust lifting from the earth and heard the swearing of men and the harsh, painful grunts of a horse that is being savagely spurred and whipped.

Clint dismounted and tied the burro to a piece of brush. He moved swiftly toward the dust and the noise keeping himself behind a low ridge. When the ridge petered out, he flattened on the ground and crawled forward until he saw the ranch and the vaquero's breaking corral.

Clint's stomach twisted as the vaquero and Duke fought each other with grim ferocity. The vaquero was obviously a masterful rider, but Clint had seen enough bronc busters to know that Escobar had been thrown many times and was now using every trick in the book to stay atop the gelding.

He had tied a rolled saddle blanket behind the cantle to lodge himself in the seat and he was wearing leather pants that were no doubt soaked with water so as to better grip saddle leather. But worst of all, and completely unforgivable, the rowels of his terrible spurs were locked so that they were like meat hooks. Seeing the bloody welts on Duke's flanks, Clint's lips pulled back in a snarl.

The Gunsmith moved quickly. He knew that the moment to strike was now, while the four Mexicans were absorbed by the fierce contest taking place. He came up behind them and could have taken them all except that the vaquero saw him and shouted a warning.

Clint's heavy staff crashed down on Manuel's head and split it open. Juan cried out as the staff flashed again and broke his wrist when his gun came up. For good measure, Clint broke the man's other arm too, then dove for the weapon even as Jose's pistol barked meanly. A bullet whined off the hard ground. Clint rolled and came up firing. Jose crashed through the vaquero's corral fence, dead before he hit the chewed up battleground. The vaquero himself was so rattled that he momentarily forgot the great horse he was riding.

A moment was all that Duke needed. He used the last of his great power to hurl his tormentor into the snubbing post buried deep in the center of the corral. Escobar struck the stout post so hard he was knocked unconscious.

Clint dropped his staff and shoved open the corral gate. He staggered inside to his horse and threw his arms around Duke's lathered neck. "It's my fault," he said. "Somehow, I'm going to find a way to make this up to you."

The gelding's head bobbed up and down.

Manuel and Jose were dead, but Clint did not kill Juan or the vaquero. Instead, he tied them up hand and foot to the corral. They would scream and holler and someone would eventually hear them and come.

Probably.

Clint was happy to have his own weapons again and he did not hesitate to also take the weapons and horses of the bandits. Bandits were nothing without horses and guns. It was like defanging a couple of lobo wolves.

"*Senor*," please!" Juan croaked. "Mercy!"

"You are alive after leaving me to die. That is my mercy," the Gunsmith said, as he turned Duke north and led the bandits' horses into the fading sunlight.

When he returned to the small burro, he gave it water from a goatskin and rubbed its muzzle. Then, he tied it to the tail of the last horse and continued toward the border.

It was late in the next afternoon when he returned to the peon's small rock hut. The old man was still working his garden just as he had been the last time the Gunsmith had seen him. The angel was standing in the doorway and she cried out happily to see him and their little burro return.

Clint dismounted stiffly. He had sold the bandits' guns and horses in Juarez for a hundred and sixty dollars. It was more money than the old peon had probably earned in ten years of growing and selling his hard-won vegetables in town.

Clint gave the old man a sack with the money and some sticks of excellent peppermint candy. The peon stared at it for a long time, and then he gave it to his daughter. Her eyes filled with tears.

"*Gracias!*" she whispered. Then, she gave each of them a stick of candy and they ate together before they said *adios*. It was Sunday and the lovely young *senorita* and her father would be going to Mass.

As he neared the border, Clint could hear the chapel bells pealing and calling the people to church. He smiled at a pretty little girl about five years old with a flower in her hair.

"*Buenas dias, Senor!*"

"*Buenas dias, Senorita!*"

She giggled. She was not a *senorita*, but Clint had forgotten the name for girl and so he had pretended to greatly flatter her.

But as Clint neared the border, he noticed that a lot of families were crossing into El Paso. In fact, hordes of families.

"What's going on?" he asked another *gringo*.

"Big horse race today! Much betting."

"Who's racing?"

"The champion of El Paso, Silver Shot, against a foul animal that hit and injured him during their last race. A red stallion by the name of Crimson Victory."

Clint blinked. He nudged Duke forward into a run and the big gelding galloped up to the Rio Grande and splashed across into Texas.

This was the race he had been waiting to see.

TWENTY-THREE

The race was ready to begin when Clint arrived. Judging from the anxious faces of the huge crowd, Clint decided that if he in any way tried to stop it, they'd tear him to pieces. So he did what any intelligent man would have done and that was to dismount and find a good place to watch.

His eyes scanned the sea of faces searching for Lola Perdue and her sister Maggie. Once, he thought that he had seen them, but when he blinked they were gone, and he could not be sure it had not been two other women. Clint did not become overly concerned. This just might be the biggest horse race staged in Texas, and he would bet that Lola and Maggie would be here ready to collect their winnings.

Down at the end of the race course he could see Rosie and Crimson Victory being led to the starting line. He also saw a big, powerful looking dapple gray and he remembered that its name was Silver Shot.

"If that red bastard wins," a spectator snarled, "this crowd will roast him and that woman jockey!"

Clint heard a low murmur of agreement. The atmosphere was nothing like the usual one you'd find at a race, but instead, it was grim and dangerous.

"The best horse ought to win," Clint said. "Didn't the red beat the gray once already?"

He knew that it had.

"Hell yes, but only because the girl let it injure Silver Shot! Most of us lost a bundle on that race. By God, it had better not happen that way again!"

"Here we go," Clint said, hearing the crowd hush. He strained to see down the long road that served as a racetrack. He wondered what Rosie was feeling and thinking. No matter, when she crossed the finish line, win, lose or draw, he was going to get her out of this mess that she had gotten herself into. It would probably mean a year or two in prison, but that sure beat a lifetime of running scared or being strung up by a lynch mob.

Rosie was tough. She could take a short prison term if it had to be that way in the eyes of the courts. The main thing was getting her clear of Lola Perdue before that woman totally corrupted her.

Rosie was scared to death. She knew the mood of the crowd and what it would do to her and Crimson Victory if they won. If she won she lost, if she lost she won. It made no sense at all. The only thing that counted was to let the race take place and let the best horse win.

Rosie believed that the gray was the better horse, but she had been exercising the red stallion all week and Crimson Victory had never run so fast. Maybe she really could win. It deserved to try. She was going to let the horse run as fast as it could.

This time, the animals were kept far apart. There would be no fighting between the stallions and no potential for injury.

"All right!" the starter yelled as the two thorough-breds were led prancing toward the line. "Riders and horses ready!"

Rosie nodded. She leaned over the neck of her horse and wrapped her fingers into the stallion's thick mane. She saw the starter raise his gun and then the handlers jumped aside. Clint saw a puff of white gunsmoke an instant before he heard the weapon crack sharply. The tall running horses jumped forward and sprinted down the dirt road running shoulder to shoulder.

Rosie hung tight. She neither whipped her mount nor did she urge it to run faster. She knew this horse would give it everything and that it wanted to win. Beside her, she could feel the gray stallion and the road seemed a blur underneath their pounding hooves. The crowd was just a smear of color. Rosie's senses became especially acute. She smelled dry grass, dust and cigar smoke wafting. She concentrated on the power of the animal between her legs.

The gray stallion began to pull away a little. Rosie willed the red to run faster. Despite her decision not to interfere, she found herself urging Crimson Victory, "Come on! You can take him, come on!"

The red stretched and closed the gap at the mile marker. But the gray again made a surge at the mile and a quarter marker and the crowd was going insane with joy.

"Come on!" Rosie yelled. She slapped the red smartly across the rump and the animal threw itself forward again. It began to close but all of a sudden, they were running out of race and then, just as the horse beneath her flung itself at the gray, they shot across the finish line.

The gray stallion of El Paso had won by a nose.

Rosie was crying as she slowly pulled Crimson Victory in and the crowd roared with elation. A huge

mob raced toward the gray and its jockey and Rosie
saw the little man being pulled off his horse and lifted
high overhead. Rosie looked ahead down the empty
road and wanted more than anything in the world to
keep going. But she couldn't leave Maggie. They had
become friends. The girl needed her strength. Needed
some hope. They would soon escape Lola Perdue and
everything would be all right.

She dropped down to the hard road, suddenly feeling a tremendous sense of relief. The crowd would
have crucified them had they won this second race.
"It's going to be all right," Rosie told the trembling
thoroughbred as she stroked its muzzle. "Another
hundred feet and you'd have beat that animal. You
were fixin' to pass him by. You're the best horse. It's
all right."

Rosie walked her animal to cool it down. She felt
better than she had in a long, long while. The race
had been fair and it had been a tremendous effort on
the part of both of the magnificent stallions. She did
not know how Lola Perdue had bet all of their previous winnings and she really did not care.

A horse galloped up to stop beside her. "Rosie?"
She spun around. "Clint!"

He dropped from his horse and she threw herself
into his arms. "I came to get you out of this mess,"
he said as he held her tight. "I came to take you back
to face justice, but I'll do everything in my power to
see that your sentence is light."

She stiffened. Pushed back from him. "I can't go,
Clint. I'd die locked up in prison."

"You stole horses, helped Lola escape jail in Ft.
Worth. You were there when they set the people of
Big Spring up for a bank robbery that took their savings. I don't know what else you've done, but . . .
you can't expect to just walk away scot-free."

"I've done enough wrong for a lifetime. But I'm in

this now, and I have also saved a few lives that would have been lost had I not been with Lola. And there's little Maggie. She's not a real criminal. She's just confused and afraid to defy her big sister.''

"Maggie is a woman. You both are and you have to be held accountable for what you've done." Clint hated himself for this, but better he took them in now than waited until someone killed Rosie, or until she gunned down some innocent bystander during a bank robbery, who foolishly tried to play hero.

Rosie nodded. "I know you are right but . . . but Clint, I'd rather be dead than locked up!"

"You have to face the music or the dance is gonna stop for you forever—at the end of a gun, or a rope."

Rosie took a deep breath and nodded. "What about Lola and Maggie?"

"We'll go find them right now," Clint said.

"But will they hang Maggie? Clint, it's not the same with those two. Lola is evil, but Maggie isn't!"

He nodded. He wanted more than anything in the world to say that a court or a jury would take everything into consideration and that Maggie would be forgiven the deaths that the Perdue sisters had caused. But that would be lying and he could not lie. If Lola was sentenced to death, Maggie would also be.

"Let's just do what we can. You can testify for Maggie and I'll put in my two bits as well."

"I suppose that's the best we can do."

He nodded. "Yeah."

They mounted and rode back toward the biggest celebration that El Paso had known in years. But neither Clint nor Rosie were smiling at the laughter. All the Gunsmith wanted to do was to find the Perdue sisters and get the hell back to Ft. Worth.

TWENTY-FOUR

Clint dismounted and handed Duke's reins to Rosie. "I think it would be better if I hunted them on foot," he said. "On horseback they'd be sure to spot me first and run. Either that, or they'd put a bullet into me."

Rosie shook her head. "You have nothing to fear from Maggie. But Lola, she'd kill you in the bat of an eye."

Clint had known that already. He plunged into the huge crowd and began the search. There were several thousand people here and it was not going to be easy to spot Lola and her sister, but he knew they would be here somewhere amidst this hard drinking, hard celebrating bunch of Texans.

Ten minutes later, he saw Lola Perdue. She was wearing a white bonnet with pink ribbons, and he would have recognized her earlier if the bonnet and the parasol she was holding did not partially obscure her face. For some reason, she looked stricken and slightly dazed. There was a huge throng of irate bettors around her and Clint saw that they were demanding money.

Lola was obviously in great difficulty. She was shaking her head and trying to explain something that they obviously did not appreciate.

Clint took a deep breath. Maggie was not in sight and that posed a problem because Lola would require all of his attention. He decided he would simply tell the crowd of demanding bettors that the law took precedence over their gambling claims. Maybe, given the obvious graveness of her circumstances, Lola would even come peaceably.

Clint strode forward with a determined set to his lean jaw. He was not a law officer anymore and, if there was trouble, he could not pull out a badge and simply make an arrest. But he was a citizen and he could apprehend a known criminal. Sheriff Coddington might raise a mighty big squawk about the reward money, but Clint hoped to have the three women spirited out of town before he even realized they were finally in his grasp.

It was almost over.

But suddenly, from out of the corner of his eye, Clint caught a threatening movement. Years of being a lawman had sharpened his instincts for survival and that was all that saved his life as two men lunged at him with knives. It happened so fast that Clint could do nothing but drop to his knees. His move was pure reaction and the two killers were unable to check their forward momentum. Clint's ribs caught them below the knees and they crashed headfirst into the crowd.

A woman screamed, her voice shrill and terror-filled. Clint drew his gun and shot both knife men in the shoulder before they could reach back their arms and make their deadly throws. He started toward

Lola when a tall, scar-faced man lunged at him with a huge Bowie knife.

Clint felt its blade rip through his shirt and glance off his ribs. He grunted with pain, locked his hands on the man's wrist and they crashed to the ground rolling and fighting to control the knife as the crowd scattered.

Then, out of nowhere, Clint had a momentary glimpse of Lola Perdue's hate-filled face. He saw the derringer in her fist and knew that he was powerless to defend himself. He was going to die.

But Lola bent close and hissed at the scar-faced man, "Betrayer!" What happened next seemed like a miracle. Instead of putting a bullet through the Gunsmith's heart, she turned it on the man in Clint's grasp and pulled the trigger.

Clint felt the man's powerful body stiffen. He saw Lola drop the gun between them and heard her scream, "He's murdered Mr. Raymond. He's murdered poor Mr. Bart Raymond!"

It was done so fast and so beautifully that the shocked crowd believed Lola. And if there were a few who saw that the derringer was in her fist and not Clint's, they decided their eyes were playing tricks on them. Lola Perdue disappeared as Sheriff Coddington pulled Clint off the dead racehorse owner.

"You're under arrest for murder!" he proclaimed.

Clint shook his head. "But I didn't kill him!"

"Tell that to the jury, if I can get you to jail before a lynch mob hoists you into a tree!"

Clint grabbed his cut and bleeding ribs. He was dizzy and the pain was so great it assailed him like huge, rolling waves that threatened to drown his senses. He did not understand why Lola had murdered the man named Raymond, but she had done him no real favor. He believed he could have

torn the Bowie knife from the man's grasp and subdued him. But now he was going to jail charged with
murdering the most popular man in El Paso this race
day.

"Clint!"

He managed to raise his head and look up at Rosie
sitting astride the beaten Crimson Victory. She could
say nothing, but she seemed to nod her head. What
did that mean? That she would help him? Or that she
was happy he would no longer be dogging her outlaw
trail?

"Murderer!" someone yelled. Clint was rocked by
a fist as the mob tried to tear him out of the sheriff's
grasp.

He passed out on his feet thinking he would probably never wake up again in this world.

TWENTY-FIVE

It was nighttime when Clint awoke and there was a large bandage around his chest reminding him of his knife wound. He surveyed the dim interior of the cell and then ground his teeth against the pain as he eased his boots to the rock floor and shuffled to the bars.

"Water," he said. "I need a drink of water."

Sheriff Coddington was sound asleep in his office chair, feet propped up on his desk. At Clint's voice, he stopped snoring and rubbed his eyes. "Huh? What . . . oh," he growled, "it's only you."

Clint gripped the bars and shook them. "Water! Give me a drink of water or you'll not go back to sleep this night!"

Coddington swore softly. His heavy boots thunked to the floor and he stumbled half-asleep over to the water bucket. He took a battered metal dipper and filled it to the brim. He splashed water all the way across the floor to the cell.

"You drink and then you shut up," he said. "You

already caused me enough trouble for one day."

Clint drank. The water cooled his parched throat and cleared his fevered mind. "How come you did it?"

"What?"

"Kept the mob from hanging me?"

"That's my job," the lawman said with a grin. "The fact that you killed Bart Raymond and solved a hell of a big problem for me also had something to do with it."

"I didn't kill the man. Lola Perdue did."

Coddington's expression went crafty. "I could believe that. Possibly, Raymond set the Perdue woman up in Juarez, Mexico, for a double cross on that horse race. Supposin' the man even told her that he would have his horse drugged to lose. Hearing that, she'd have bet heavily—everything she'd won on that first race—on her own horse and it lost. That's why Lola probably wanted him dead."

Clint smiled thinly. "You and I know that there's no supposin', or possibilities about any of this. She was double-crossed and she killed him right in the middle of a crowd."

The sheriff just shrugged. "You have no proof to support any of what we've just talked about. I'd say your chances of going to prison are about dead certain."

Clint turned around for he did not want the man to see his bitterness. He was trapped thanks to Lola Perdue who had killed one enemy and was about to send the other to prison. The woman had defeated both he and Bart Raymond. And now, she was probably miles away and heading for some new town to fleece.

"Say, Sheriff?"

"Yeah?"

"Since we both know I'm innocent, what's it going

to take to get me out of here?"

"A verdict of innocent which you will not receive," the man said happily. "You see, Gunsmith, I warned you to split the Perdue woman's reward with me. But you got greedy and wanted it all to yourself. That was a big mistake."

"You're making an even bigger one if you don't help me escape."

Sheriff Coddington's voice roughened. "Don't threaten me," he warned. "I am the law in El Paso and now that Raymond is gone, I damn sure don't have to answer to anyone except the voters on election day."

"You," Clint said, sitting down heavily on his bunk, "are a disgrace to the law profession."

"Shut up," Coddington said without rancor. "I'm losing my beauty sleep."

Clint eased back onto his thin straw mattress and stared up at the black ceiling of his cell. He was in one hell of a bad fix for every one of the following reasons: He had gotten sliced with a very sharp Bowie knife; Lola Perdue and her sister were no doubt fleeing the city and their trail would run cold again; Rosie was probably with them; and most immediate, he was stuck here in jail facing very hostile El Paso citizens who were dead certain he had killed Bart Raymond!

Things did not look good.

Nothing improved the following week during the jury selection and from the gossip Clint overheard, he was as good as convicted already. There were said to be a hundred men ready to swear that they had seen the fight and then heard the gunshot with which Clint had killed Bart Raymond. Never mind that Raymond had attacked the Gunsmith. Hadn't he just shot and seriously wounded two other men? Altogether, that meant three men either dead or wounded in less than three violent minutes.

The word spoken on the streets and in the shops was that the famous Gunsmith had gone over the edge and was now a danger and clear menace to society. Why, it was nothing short of a miracle that one of his bullets had not strayed and killed some innocent bystander!

Clint had to bite back his tongue in order not to comment. All three had attacked him, goddammit! And he would never have fired in a crowd if he had not been sure of his shots. It had been no miracle that he had wounded the first two knifers who had attacked him.

"I think you'll hang unless I find someone to testify that they saw you attacked," the sherrif said the night before the trial was to begin.

Clint frowned. "Find somebody? What are you trying to pull, anyway?"

"Nothing. I just figured that if you pleaded guilty, but guilty in the act of self-defense, we could save us and the town a lot of trouble. You'd get . . . oh, fifteen or twenty years in prison . . . with the possibility of an early parole for good behavior."

The Gunsmith laughed outright. "I don't believe I'm hearing this," he said. "You're telling me you'll find a witness to back up my self-defense testimony if I plead guilty to a lesser charge?"

"That's the way it'd work," Coddington said. "Besides, it was self-defense."

"So why don't you say that under oath?"

"Because," the sheriff said, "I want you out of the way for a good long while. So have we got a deal? You can choose a long vacation in prison instead of a rope."

Clint gripped the bars. "I'm going to testify to this conversation," he vowed. "I'll tell them about your offer. Even if I go to the gallows, I'll still make them think twice about voting for you on election day!"

Coddington jumped to his feet and pulled his gun. Shaking with fury, he charged over to the cell and pointed his weapon at Clint. "I ought to kill you and say you was trying to escape!"

Clint backed to the wall, fully expecting to be shot. But Coddington's nerve broke and he shoved the gun back into his holster and slammed out of the office heading for a saloon and a drink.

"Whew," Clint said, feeling his knees begin to rattle. "I'd better not goad him anymore. He's about ready to explode."

A voice from just outside the window said, "I agree. Good luck, Gunsmith. Please don't try to follow me. I couldn't survive in prison any more than you could."

And then, a six-gun dropped through the window and landed on the mattress.

Clint jumped up too suddenly and felt a small tear of flesh over his ribs. He grunted in pain but whispered, "Rosie! Rosie, wait!"

But the sound of galloping hooves told him that she was gone.

Clint sat down on his mattress and inspected the weapon. It was in good working order and loaded. If he had not heard Rosie's voice with his own ears, he would have suspected Coddington of a trick to get him to attempt a break so that he could shoot him down in the street.

But he had heard Rosie. And the gun in his fist was as good as a key to his cell door. Clint slipped the gun under his blanket and lifted his shirt to inspect his wound. He had opened it up a little, but not much. A small amount of fresh blood told him he must be more careful.

"Come on sheriff," he said, tightening his bandages. "Before she gets fifty miles away on that red stallion. Before her trail disappears again."

TWENTY-SIX

It was sometime after midnight when Clint heard the angry rumble of the crowd as it burst from a nearby saloon to tumble out into the street. Clint had heard that sound before and it had always made the hairs on the back of his neck stand on end. It was the drunken, kill-crazed noise of a slavering lynch mob.

Of course, the Gunsmith thought grimly. Sheriff Coddington could not afford to have me up on the witness stand telling the court about his role in this mess. How he tried to make a deal in order to keep me quiet.

Clint took a deep breath and slipped the six-gun down into the top of his right boot. He pulled his trousers over the boots and even though he would not be able to get at the concealed weapon quickly, there was no other place he could hide it that the approaching lynch mob would not quickly discover.

He swallowed and gripped the bars, feeling the palms of his hands grow slick with perspiration. At least five times during his long career as a lawman,

mobs had tried to storm the jail and lynch one of his
prisoners. Usually, the accused deserved rope justice
but Clint had always stood before the mob and
defended his prisoner with his own life if need be. It
was part of a sheriff's job and one that he swore to
uphold when he assumed office. Often, it was the
hardest thing in the world to do—face down your
neighbors and friends and take the side of some cold-
blooded killer. But the law was the law.

The crowd struck the front door and he heard
Sheriff Coddington plead weakly, "I sure wish you
men would let the court decide whether he hangs or
not."

"The hell with the court!" the crowd roared, as
the door flew open.

Clint felt a cold river of fear shoot down his back-
bone as the drunken saloon crowd poured into the
office and grabbed the cell door keys. He saw one
man standing with a rope in his hand, and it wasn't
even a hangman's noose that would mercifully break
his neck. Hell no, this man had fashioned nothing
more than an ordinary loop that would strangle a
man slowly so that he would kick and choke a long,
long time.

"I warn you," Coddington yelled once more just
to make it look good, "this is against the law and you
are all guilty!"

"To hell with the law! Everybody saw him shoot
Bart Raymond! The court is a waste of the taxpayers'
money!"

A big, full-bearded man jammed the key to Clint's
cell into the lock and twisted it open. "You coming
out easy or hard?" he asked with a malicious grin.

"Hard," Clint said. "Come and take me."

The man liked that idea fine. He swore and lunged
and Clint kicked him in the crotch. The man

screamed and went to the floor as the mob rushed in. Clint stood back to the wall and fought them with every bit of his strength. He punched, kicked and battled like a cornered cat, but their sheer weight and numbers finally brought him down. Half unconscious, he was dragged from the cell and through the office. He caught a glimpse of the sheriff and the man was almost smiling.

Clint had known that if he pulled his six-gun while in the jail he would kill a few men, but that they would surely kill him, too. But if he could get outdoors on a horse, he still might have a chance to see tomorrow's sunrise.

They were hooting and howling like savages as they bore him down the street toward a big tree that had, no doubt, seen more than its share of men dancing at the end of a rope.

Now that he was outside, the Gunsmith relaxed and let the crowd carry him along.

"Get him a horse!" someone yelled. "Any damned horse will do for what we got in mind! He ain't going to ride more than three feet!"

The crowd thought this was the funniest damned thing that they had heard all night and they howled uproariously.

Clint was thrown on a horse and, to his relief, it looked like a decent enough animal. He was led by men with torches until he came to rest under the tree.

Sheriff Coddington said, "Boys, I can't stop what's going to happen here tonight and I guess I have to say that I don't blame anyone. Bart Raymond was one of El Paso's best known citizens and he owned Silver Shot, the fastest damned horse in Texas!"

Bottles were raised and cheers made but their tongues fell silent as they watched the Gunsmith.

Clint sat grim in the saddle. His face was bloodied and numb from the battle he'd put up back in the cell. His hard glare fixed on all of them and they avoided his eyes.

"You got any last words?" a man asked quietly.

"Yeah." The Gunsmith spat blood. "I got some you all ought to hear. Your sheriff is a crook and a coward. He knows full well that it was Lola Perdue who killed Raymond. And even if it had been me, since when is it a hanging offense to protect your own life after someone comes after you with a Bowie knife?"

No one answered him and Clint went on, his words striking them like the tip of a bullwhip. "This is one of the most cowardly deeds that ever took place in Texas. Tomorrow when you are sober, you'll remember my words and be too ashamed to even look each other in the eye."

They shifted uneasily.

"Sheriff," Clint challenged, "I want you to show this mob what a coward you really are by refusing to put the rope over my head and bind my hands behind my back. Come on, let's see if you have the stomach for it!"

All eyes turned to the sheriff and it was clear he was repelled. But Clint had thrown down the challenge and he knew that he could not back down now.

"All right," he stammered, as he took a step forward, "all right! By God, I'll show you what kind of a man I am."

"You already have," Clint said in a cold voice. He waited until the sheriff was beside the horse and then, Clint reached down and pulled the six-gun out of his boot top. In almost the same motion, he dropped out of the saddle and wrapped his arm around Coddington's neck. It was done so fast that the drunken

crowd had no chance at all to react. Clint put his
back to the horse.

The sheriff tried to cry out but Clint's strong arm
choked off his words. He shoved the gun up against
the man's skull and yelled, "One mistake and I'll
blow Coddington's brains out!"

The mob froze.

"All right," Clint gritted through clenched teeth.
"I think you folks ought to know that this man and
Bart Raymond were pardners in about every crooked
scheme ever thought up in this town. You don't
believe that? How much do you pay him? Thirty,
forty, even fifty dollars a month! Take a look at his
bank account tomorrow and see what he's worth! He
could buy any of you from the last two horse races
alone that he and Raymond rigged."

Clint nudged the point of his gun against the man's
head. "Tell them the deal you offered me earlier this
evening or say good-bye to this world."

Coddington babbled like a brook. Then Clint
made him tell them how it really was Lola Perdue
who had killed Raymond. And how he and Raymond
had worked out several deals to their great advantage. Clint made the man sing like a bird. And when
he was through, Clint hurled him at the mob.

"Where's my black gelding!" he snapped.

"He's at Wilson's Livery. I'll go get him," a man
offered apologetically.

"The hell with you," Clint snapped as he wiped his
battered face. He grabbed the rope from a man's
grasp and hurled it to the ground. "This is the kind
of justice that I spent years trying to wipe out. Take
this . . . this pathetic excuse for a lawman back and
lock him in his own jail! Demand to see his bank account and send him to prison where he belongs."

"Might be we should hang him instead of you," a

big man wearing a red plaid shirt hissed.

Clint remembered him in the jail cell and the Gunsmith's fist traveled upward to connect with the point of the man's jaw and drop him in the dirt.

"Some men never learn unless they have sense beaten into them," the Gunsmith said with disgust.

He left the mob standing under the tree and he hoped they'd think long and hard about how they had almost hung an innocent man.

Clint found Duke in a stall and saddled him quickly. El Paso was a bad taste in his mouth right now, and he wanted to put some distance between himself and this hard Texas town.

He had no idea where he'd find Rosie and knew that the roads going in and out were so well traveled it would probably be impossible to find Crimson Victory's hoofprints.

The Gunsmith's fingers strayed to his shirt pocket and he brought out a bent twig that served as a measure of the red thoroughbred's hoof. A twig. It sure wasn't much to go on.

Clint rode out of town and past the lynch mob who watched him from the street. One fool even yelled out that he was sorry. Another drunken fool wished the Gunsmith good luck.

To hell with them all. Clint rolled the twig straight between his thumb and forefinger. He was going to find Rosie on that red race horse if he had to ride a thousand miles.

TWENTY-SEVEN

The trail had gone stone cold in New Mexico three months before and Clint had ridden a thousand miles in the hunt for Rosie and the Perdue women. There had been no more bank robberies, and Clint wondered if that was because Rosie had put her foot down and refused to be involved. The Gunsmith hoped so. Bank robberies would get people killed almost every time.

From what Clint had managed to piece together, Lola Perdue had decided to stick to their game of winning horse races. And there were plenty. Rosie and Crimson Victory were hitting every little town and community in New Mexico and West Texas. There were no more big races like the one in El Paso. Instead, the three women had apparently decided to race in small matches that were unlikely to create much attention.

They had colored the red thoroughbred's shiny coat, too. Before arriving in some towns, they painted spots on his rump so that he was described as an appaloosa. At other towns, they powdered his coat so that he looked like a true strawberry roan.

But what they could not do was change the fact that the horse was owned, ridden and handled by three women, two of which were extraordinarily good looking. So, even though they might disguise Crimson Victory, the word was spreading about the three women and match races were getting more difficult to find.

Now, as Clint stopped before the Townsend Livery, in Seminole, Texas, he heard the same story that he had heard more and more as of late.

"Yep," the livery owner said, chewing on a stem of alfalfa hay, "they was through Seminole just a week or so ago. Three women and a tall gray stallion. Only it wasn't really gray, the son of a bitch was powdered up."

"How do you know that?" Clint asked, letting his horse drink from the man's water trough.

" 'Cause it was a damn hot day and the thoroughbred was sweatin' just a little around the flanks. I could see how the sweat washed out the powder."

"Did they race here?"

"Judge Kilburn has a little buckskin mare that is mighty fast. He wanted to race their horse but for only a half mile."

"And?"

"They wouldn't hear of it. Said their horse needed a mile just to hit its full stride. They wanted a mile and a half. So no race."

The liveryman scratched his protruding belly. "I heard a rumor about three women and a fast horse. Got beat down in El Paso, though, didn't he?"

"He sure did," Clint said. "By another thoroughbred named Silver Shot and also by this horse of mine."

The man looked at Duke with new appreciation. "I'd have to see it to believe it," he said after a long pause. "Though that is one hell of an animal you're riding. Wanta sell him?"

"Nope. Do you know which way they went?"

The man shook his head. "Nope and even if I did, I wouldn't tell you."

"Why?"

"Them woman did little Johnny Fry's mother a good turn. The widow Fry lives out on a farm about three miles east of here. Them women came by and asked for some supper. They et and when it came time to pay the widow and she asked them fo' a dollar, why they give her five! I sure wouldn't mind someone doin' that sort of thing to me some day. Widow was mighty grateful and told everybody. Was those three and that tall thoroughbred to come through Seminole again, they'd be mighty welcome by everybody in this town."

"One of them is a cold-blooded killer," Clint said patiently. "An extra four dollars sure don't buy back the wrong of taking innocent lives."

The liveryman's eyes shuttered. "Maybe not," he said, "but I believe the widow Fry and I don't know you from Adam."

Clint took the wanted poster with Lola's picture on it and shoved it out at arm's length for the livery man to see. "Now do you believe me?"

The man peered closely at it. "Can't read," he said with a shrug.

"It says she was wanted for murder, horse thieving and bank robbery."

"Maybe it does . . . maybe it doesn't, stranger."

Clint gripped his saddlehorn trying not to lose his temper with this stubborn idiot. "Well you can plainly see her face and you can see that she is now worth a thousand dollars by reading the figure, can't you?''

The man stared at the poster. He shrugged. "That picture don't do billy-be-damned for her. The woman I saw was twice that good lookin'. This'n might be someone else entirely.''

Clint reined Duke away from the water trough and with his teeth clenched, he rode on out of Seminole. What could you do with that kind of cotton-headed thinking? To try to explain that Lola was a cold-blooded killer would be a total waste of time.

But this charity business with the widow Fry was a new and very troubling complication. If Lola had decided to make herself friends in the event that she had to locate a safe refuge for hiding, it was going to make finding her a hundred times tougher.

Two hours later Clint wiped his face with a napkin and leaned back in his chair full and contented. "Mrs. Fry," he said, "that was as fine an apple pie as I ever tasted.''

The little woman beamed. She was thin and wore a plain gingham dress that once had a print of some kind but now was faded and scrubbed into obscurity. She had buckteeth and was one of the most unattractive women Clint had ever laid eyes on but she was one hell of a good cook. Some man would marry her just because she could make such terrific apple pie.

"I win the blue ribbon every year at the county fair and I know they'd like to see someone else win, but I just keep on awinnin'.''

"And you always will," the Gunsmith said expansively. "How much do I owe you?''

"Two bits for the dinner, a dime more for the two extry pieces of pie ya et.''

Clint took out a dollar. "Why don't you pack me

up the rest of the pie for the road I'm set to travel? I'll pay you a five dollars all together.''

Her hand flew to her mouth, ''My gawd!'' she cried. ''It's happened to me again! Why, Mister, you won't believe this, but just last week three ladies passed through here and paid me five dollars too!''

''How about that!'' Clint said. ''Maybe you ought to move into Seminole and open up a cafe and make a lot of money selling your pies.''

''Damn!'' she whispered, her hand starting to reach for the money and then pulling back as if she were afraid to be so bold. She found an old magazine and tore out two sheets which she used to wrap his apple pie in. Laying it down beside him on the table, she said, ''Yew really think I could?''

''I'm sure you could.''

''Damn, maybe I really should!''

Clint handed her five dollars and it quickly vanished into that faded dress. ''Mrs. Fry, I have to go on now. But first, I'd like you to tell me about those three women. Ah, do you know where they were heading?''

The woman's facial expression went from happy to hostile as fast as a man could snap his fingers. ''Why you askin'?'' she challenged.

''Just curious. I think I might even know them.''

She had a thin, rat face and now it twisted up around her nose and she hissed. ''Yew must be that fella that Miss Perdue took me aside and warned me about. Yew're the one they call the Gunsmith, ain't ya!''

Clint stood up. ''I am but—''

''Get outa my house, you sneakin' varmit! Out! And I'll jest keep your damn old money to show you what I think of a damned old sneaky!''

Clint shook his head as he retreated. ''Mrs. Fry, that woman is a killer. I need to catch her before more banks are robbed, more innocent people are killed.''

"Yew the one that's atryin' to kill her! She told me all about you and I swore I'd put a bullet in you myself if you came around and now . . . now you et my pie, set at my table and goddammit, where's my shotgun!''

Clint saw her head for the other room and that was enough for him. He leapt for the door, took five running steps and flung himself into the saddle and lined Duke out of the farmyard running like a streak. He heard the blast of a shotgun but he was safely out of range.

Clint let his horse run a full mile before he pulled the animal in and then dismounted. He tightened a loose cinch and wiped the sweat from his brow.

If Lola was going to start turning the whole countryside against him, it was sure going to make things difficult.

Clint shook his head. And he had been so rattled by Mrs. Fry's sudden ferocity that he had even forgotten to grab his extra apple pie.

"Duke," he said, "we are going to have to start treading on thin ice from now on. That woman has set her mind on making herself mighty popular. And there's only one reason I can think of that would make her do that. She knows I'm on her trail and that I won't quit until I have her either swinging from a rope, or locked up in prison where she will surely stay until she is old and ugly.''

The gelding bobbed its head. They were riding through two-foot-high grass. It was golden brown and waving in a slight afternoon breeze. Clint admired it for a minute and then he blinked. "Well, I'll be damned. Sure looks like four horses have passed through here.''

Clint dismounted and let Duke chew grass. The

Gunsmith pulled out the bent twig from his shirt
pocket and his pocketknife from his pants. He spent
a quarter hour cutting the grass down low and then
he used his twig to measure the width and length of
the clearest tracks he could find.

He found Crimson Victory's hoofprint on the
third try. Clint stood up and gazed north where the
waving grass seemed to beckon. North toward Ama-
rillo and the Texas Panhandle country.

He climbed back on the gelding and let the horse
into a nice, easy gallop that would cover a lot of miles
before dark. Big clouds boiled out of the horizon
and he saw a bolt of lightning as it scorched down
through the hot air ahead. This was his kind of country, tough but ruggedly beautiful.

Comanche had ruled this part of Texas for untold
centuries and no wonder they fought so damned hard
to protect it, first from the Kiowa and eastern
Apache, later from the white man.

But right now, Clint's thoughts centered on Lola
Perdue. That evil woman had never had a man on her
trail the way he was on it. He had the tenacity of a
bulldog in the way he would bite onto something and
just hang on until it either gave up or gave away.

"Sooner or later," he muttered as he galloped
across the hills, "I'm going to find and get you, Lola.
You got my word on it."

TWENTY-EIGHT

Lola Perdue collected the winnings that totaled up to nearly two hundred dollars. She thanked every one of the losers and when she had their attention, she climbed onto her horse and said, "Ladies and gentlemen, all of you citizens of Broken Rock, I want to thank you for a most pleasurable afternoon of racing. That sorrel mare of yours is a sure enough race horse and it gave my thoroughbred a real run for his money."

"But not enough of a run!" the mayor shouted good-naturedly. "So it was not only a pleasurable afternoon for you three, but a profitable one as well!"

The crowd muttered their agreement.

Lola smiled harmlessly. "I've heard that you folks are trying to raise money for a schoolhouse. Is that right?"

The crowd yelled and nodded.

"Good," Lola shouted back. "We'd like to donate fifty dollars for the good of your fine children!"

The crowd broke into excited applause and when they fell silent, Lola added, "We just hope that, should we ever pass through this way again, you might show us the same kind of hospitality that you did today."

The mayor bellowed, "Stick around and we'll show you some more!"

"Can't do it," Lola yelled, "but maybe next time."

She nodded to Maggie and Rosie and said in a voice so low that only they could hear, "I got a funny feeling that we are being closed in by someone. I think we had better get out of town and cover some country."

So they rode out leaving the people of Broken Rock, Texas waving them good-bye.

"She must be going soft inside," Rosie whispered to Maggie as they fell back a little because Lola liked to ride out in front.

"I don't understand it," Maggie said. "Something is wrong and has her spooked real bad. She's like a bomb ready to go off and somebody is going to get hurt."

Rosie looked back toward Broken Rock and immediately thought of the Gunsmith. Had he ignored her plea when she slipped him that gun in the El Paso jail? If so, he would be wanting to arrest them all and she had not changed her mind even a little about going to prison. What it all added up to was that they were running out of time and Texas.

"Maggie, tonight I'm going to tell her it's finished. That we are either going to buy that Nevada mustang ranch, or we're leaving her."

"I wish you wouldn't do that."

But Rosie's mind was made up. "I've been a fool not to have made that decision a long, long ways back on the trail," she said, as she watched the woman riding up ahead of her.

If nothing else, Rosie had always been brutally honest with herself. She was growing as weak and afraid of Lola as Maggie. There was something insidious about Lola Perdue. She sort of worked a spell over your mind until, one day, you woke up frightened and as submissive as a lamb being led to slaughter.

I'll put it right on the line tonight, she thought to herself with all the resolve she could muster. We must have enough money and either we go mustanging or we are going to wind up in prison.

It has to end tonight.

It was well after dark and the stars were out. They had made camp in a low place where their small fire could not be seen. Lola, as always when they slept on the ground instead of in a hotel, was in a nasty mood.

"This is no life for a woman," she complained as she nipped at a bottle of whiskey.

Rosie glanced at Maggie but the girl looked away quickly. Maggie would be of no help whatsoever, but then, Rosie had known that from the start.

"You're right," she told Lola. "It's time we ended all this and headed straight for Nevada."

Lola glanced up from the campfire and her face hardened. "I say when we leave Texas, not you!"

"I'm leaving in the morning," Rosie said in as firm a voice as she could muster. "With Maggie."

She had a gun on her shapely hip and she figured she could use it as well as Lola. The woman was only deadly when she had you charmed or off your guard.

"Maggie? Ha! She's my sister! Maggie, you tell this fool that we Perdue women stick together no matter what."

Crouched down beside the fire, Maggie looked small and afraid. Like a field mouse. She could not summon up the nerve to look at her sister, but she said, "I'm tired of this. Please, I want to go with Rosie to Nevada. You promised a long time ago."

Rosie tensed. She felt a shot of adrenaline coursing through her veins and also a big jolt of pride at Maggie's unexpected courage. The gauntlet had been hurled down between them. If Lola was going to try and kill her, this would be the time and the place.

But Lola was as unpredictable as ever. Instead of reacting with violence, she clasped her hands in her lap and said, "So, the vote is two to my one." She shrugged. "Okay, I guess we head for Nevada."

Rosie sagged with relief and Maggie smiled and nodded. "Tomorrow, right?"

"Sure. Why not? But, ah . . . we do need more cash. Quite a bit more cash."

"We can do a few more races along the way," Rosie said.

"Uh-uh," Lola said. "We've run out of towns. We are like pebbles thrown into a pond. The ripples have gone out too far in all directions and it doesn't work anymore."

"But we won two hundred dollars today!" Rosie said.

"No we didn't. You see, I had to give five to one odds because of our reputations. And didn't either one of you notice that newspaper reporter who was pestering me? I'm afraid we are becoming celebrities. He was from Austin and wanted to do a story on us."

"That's crazy," Rosie said, growing pale with worry. "We wouldn't last a week! One big story and half the lawmen in Texas would be after us."

"I know that as well as anyone. That's why I agree that this game is over. I think that we are already being followed by more than one newspaperman."

Rosie nodded. So that was who the woman feared was following them.

Lola shook her head. "We only made a few dollars and I gave most of that away for the school."

"What are you getting at?" Rosie asked bluntly.

"Just that we need one more holdup."

"No."

"Yes!" Lola turned toward her sister. "Maggie, I swear there will be no killing this time. Just this once more and then we'll take the money and that will be the end of it."

"But . . ."

"Listen," Lola said urgently, "we have to do it!"

"Not me," Rosie said. "I'll have no part of it."

"Me neither," Maggie said, her voice low and stretched to the breaking point.

"Then I'll do it alone! Will you at least hold my horse in the alley behind the bank?"

Rosie started to shake her head. But Maggie broke and said, "Yes."

I'm trapped, Rosie thought. I can't leave Maggie to do it alone.

"What about you?" Lola asked. "Are you with Maggie and I, or against us?"

"I'll help Maggie with the horses," Rosie said bitterly, "but no gunplay."

"No gunplay," Lola said, visibly relaxing. "One last job and then we ride for Nevada."

So it was decided. Rosie lay back on her blankets. She saw a shooting star burn a white arc across the indigo heavens. Maybe that meant they would have good luck this last time. Maybe they'd find a small bank and all its employees would meekly give in to Lola's demands and there would be no killing.

Maybe but I doubt it, she thought, wishing on the bright North Star.

TWENTY-NINE

The little cattle town of Cut 'N Run, Texas had the look of prosperity and that was because many of the local ranchers had just returned from the railroad trailheads to the north. With their big longhorn herds sold, the ranchers had come home with their saddlebags stuffed with cash. A lot of it had already been spent on payrolls, winter feed, and old debts, but a lot of it also went straight into the bank of Cut 'N Run.

When Clint rode into town, the nip of fall was in the air. Trees were turning color, and leaves were starting to float down and drift along the street. He knew he was closing in on Rosie and the Perdue women. In each town, he had learned something new and the trail was now very fresh.

But he and Duke were dog-tired. They had made up almost a week by riding hard and late every night.

Duke's weight had dropped and Clint was as lean and as cross as a winter-starved wolf. He was weary of this hunt and ready to settle accounts.

He boarded his horse at the best looking livery in town and tipped the man who owned the place generously. Once again, the Gunsmith silently thanked Marilyn Tippett back in Ft. Worth for giving him that thousand dollars. It had sure come in handy. Not that he had spent much of it, but it was nice to be able to tip a little extra and get himself and his weary horse the best that was offered.

Clint sauntered over to the sheriff's office but it was closed and a sign in the window said the man would not return until three o'clock. That was shoddy sheriffing and Clint frowned, then headed for the nearest saloon. He had decided to give himself and his played out horse one night in town and all that went with it—a hot bath to soak away the sweat and trail dust he'd earned, a feather bed, a little whiskey to wash away more trail dust on his insides, and maybe even a woman to remind him of what they looked like. Clint had not had a woman since this whole woman-hunt had begun.

The cowboys who saw him coming along the boardwalk instinctively moved aside as he passed. Clint had a three day growth of beard, and fatigue was written into every dirt-encrusted line of his face. His gun rested on a narrow hip and he moved slow and with great weariness, but also with a hint of speed and determination.

He did not even catch the name of the saloon he walked into but when he sidled up to the bar, he leaned a boot on the brass footrail and said, "Whiskey, your best."

The bartender jumped to fill his order and when Clint tossed his drink down straight, it burned the hair off the inside of his throat, then hit the bottom of his belly and spread a nice slow fire that moved right out to his fingertips.

"Want another?"

Clint shook his head. "I'll be back after I clean up and have dinner," he said. "Any women around here?"

The man grinned. "All shapes, sizes and prices, friend!"

Clint grinned back. "Friend, I never pay. Once in awhile, they do."

The bartender laughed uproariously and started telling the other patrons Clint's joke, never realizing that it was the honest truth.

Outside, the sun was blazing and Clint turned east to find a good hotel. He was halfway down the street when he heard the first gunshot.

Spinning around, always conscious of his reputation and the many men he'd put in prison and who had sworn to kill him upon their release, Clint drew his gun.

He looked down the street and his heart sank to his feet. Lola Perdue was wounded and had dropped a satchel full of money in front of the bank. Her hair was tucked up and under her hat and she wore a man's clothes, but there was no mistaking her true identity.

Clint saw her rise to her feet, raise her gun and shoot a man who jumped into the doorway. The man pitched over grabbing his stomach.

The Gunsmith was already running but so were a lot of other men. Cut 'N Run was a hard cowboy town and every man on the street had money in that bank. Clint saw Maggie Perdue and Rosie come racing around the corner from the rear of the bank on horseback. They were leading Lola's mount but before she could reach it, a volley of gunfire knocked both women out of their saddles.

"No!" Clint shouted sprinting for Rosie.

Lola tried to raise her gun but a lucky bullet sent it

spinning. She tried to get up and reach the horses but they were running away.

Clint slammed into the side of a cowboy who was about to shoot Rosie. He knocked the man down and threw himself before the girl.

"Hold your fire!" he yelled, shielding Rosie. "Hold it!"

Two men were grabbing Lola, who was fighting and yelling for them to let go of her.

"Let her go to her sister," Clint said quietly, knowing that Maggie Perdue had died in that first volley.

Lola tore free and fell at her sister's side. She broke down and cried and it wasn't acting this time. All around them, cowboys, ranchers and merchants stood grim-faced and angry. Clint yelled for someone to get a doctor.

He looked at Rosie's wound and smiled tightly. "It's nothing that serious," he said. "Just a flesh wound."

"I'm sorry to hear that," Rosie whispered. "I wish you'd have let them kill me. I'd rather die fast than slow in a Texas prison."

Clint looked up, his eyes hard as marbles. "Hurry up with that doctor!"

"He's over seein' to Mr. Mason, our banker," a man said in a surly voice. "These women kin damn sure all bleed to death for what this town cares."

Clint looked away. He had seen enough men take bullets to know that the banker was dead.

"Rosie, Rosie," he whispered, looking down at her face. "You've really gotten yourself into a fine fix this time."

"She and this other one still alive will be hanging by the neck this time next week," the same man hissed.

Clint held Rosie close and he was never more murderous than when he looked up and whispered, "One more word, and you won't even live past a heartbeat."

The man blinked. His face flushed and he started to open his mouth but someone else grabbed his arm and yanked him away. "You goddamn fool, that's the Gunsmith!"

The man stopped resisting and hurried away.

THIRTY

The trial began the very next day. This time, there were no theatrics by Lola Perdue. The death of Maggie had left her stunned, haggard and hateful looking.

The judge called for order. "Before the court sentences these two . . . women, do they wish to say any final words that might give the court a reason to show mercy?"

Lola Perdue glared defiantly at the packed mass of spectators and hissed, "If I knew which one of you son of a bitches killed poor Maggie, I'd find a way out of jail and settle the score. My little sister never deserved to die!"

Lola's threat caused an outburst from among the spectators and the judge had to bang his gavel repeatedly before order was restored.

"Miss Rosalie Wade, do you have anything to say in your own behalf before sentencing?"

Clint looked anxiously at her as did everyone else in the room. But Rosie's head was down and she did not respond. Clint knew he had to speak for her. "Your Honor, I have something to say. Rosalie didn't rob your bank. She didn't fire a single shot at anyone. Now, I wouldn't try to say that she is without blame. After all, she and the deceased, Maggie Perdue, were holding the horses out behind the bank."

"And coming to help that one!" someone yelled, pointing an accusing finger at Lola.

Clint shook his head emphatically. "No!" he argued. "Rosie was just trying to help Maggie, not her sister. She had no gun in her hand. Neither woman did. All this court should find Rosalie Wade guilty of is for being an accessory to a crime. Nothing more."

The judge raised his eyebrows skeptically. "It has been brought to my attention that this gang has robbed other banks and swindled the citizens of New Mexico and Texas out of a great deal of money."

"Almost all of which they lost back to the citizens of El Paso." Clint raised his hands in pleading. "Judge, Lola Perdue deserves to die. She's cold-blooded and remorseless. I've seen a great many criminals in my own law career and she's as treacherous and deadly as Cattle Kate, John Wesley Hardin and Billy the Kid all rolled into one murdering package. But Rosie is innocent of all but her own gullibility. She tried to stop Lola Perdue from murdering, robbing banks and fixing horse races. She deserves clemency!"

The judge remained impassive. "Is that all?"

"Only that I would stake my name and reputation on Rosie's character and ability to go straight if given a reprieve."

"Gunsmith," the judge said, measuring his words with care, "your testimony will not go unheeded. You have a reputation of the highest order. Your per-

sonal integrity is not at question in this case. I simply
believe your heart has deceived your better judgment.
Miss Wade . . . well, she is very beautiful."

"Inside as well as out," Clint snapped.

The judge banged his gavel down hard. "This
court will take a short recess. I will deliver my verdict
when we reconvene."

Clint got up and moved toward Rosie but a pudgy,
middle-aged bailiff blocked his path. "I'm sorry,
Gunsmith, but I can't allow you to get too close to
her."

"Can we at least sit outside where it is quiet and
talk if she is handcuffed to you?"

The bailiff looked over at the sheriff who finally
nodded. "I guess that would be all right."

They moved out behind the courthouse with the
sheriff and two deputies joining them for insurance.
There were a hundred things that Clint wanted to say
to Rosie, but with her handcuffed to the bailiff, his
words and thoughts just seemed locked in his mind.

Finally, Clint expelled a deep breath and said,
"Rosie, with time off for good behavior, you could
be out of prison in seven or eight years if the judge
doesn't give you more than a twenty year sentence."

"Could you live seven or eight years in a prison
cell?"

"No," the Gunsmith admitted, thinking about
how even a day behind bars in El Paso had seemed
like an eternity.

"Neither can I, " Rosie whispered. "I might physically survive, but something inside of me would go
dead."

"I'm sorry." Clint took her hand. "I owe you one
for saving my life. They'd have rawhided me into
prison or a noose down in El Paso for the murder of
Bart Raymond."

"Clint, my dear, you really do owe me one," Rosie

said, looking him right in the eye.

Clint thought on that right up to the moment they called the court back into session.

The courtroom was silent and grim. The judge wasted no time in declaring his sentences.

"Bailiff," he ordered, "be so good as to bring the accused, Miss Lola Perdue before this bench."

Lola was pulled to her feet and she walked broodingly toward the judge. Her face was no longer beautiful, dark shadows circled her eyes and her once lovely blonde hair now hung tangled and uncombed. She looked like a prostitute who had seen her best days and was going downhill fast.

"Miss Perdue, I have no alternative but to consider the mountain of damning evidence against you. You are unquestionably guilty of murdering Mr. Arnold Mason, our banker. Furthermore, we have heard testimony and seen the wanted poster that leaves no doubt you have murdered before. You are a horse thief, a con artist and a total menace to our society. I have no choice, therefore, but to sentence you to hang by the neck until dead at this time tomorrow."

Lola threw her head back and tried to spit on the judge. She was grabbed and hustled out of the court fighting, cursing and kicking.

"Order!" the judge yelled banging his gavel. "Order in my courtroom!"

When the courtroom finally became silent again, the judge had Rosie brought before him. "Miss Rosalie Wade, I confess I have very mixed emotions concerning your degree of guilt. We have heard the Gunsmith testify as to your character and your failings. He claims your intentions were not to defend Lola Perdue. But you were wearing a gun and, in Texas, the commission of a bank robbery that involves murder is punishable by death. I therefore am required by law to sentence you to hang tomorrow alongside Miss Lola Perdue.''

''That's wrong!'' the Gunsmith shouted, coming to his feet and charging forward. ''Wrong!''

He was grabbed by the bailiff and two deputies and hauled from the room as Rosie was led back to her jail cell to await her execution.

THIRTY-ONE

It was to be the first "all woman hanging" in the world. At least that was the way the promoter hailed it when he lamented that, if the sentence had been delayed just one lousy week, he and the town of Cut 'N Run could have made a fortune in tourist dollars.

But as it was, there were only twenty-four hours to pass the word across the Texas Panhandle country of the major event. Even so, men dropped what they were doing, jumped on fast horses and rode to the little town to see the historic execution.

By nightfall, the town was filled with rowdy men drinking and carousing in anticipation of the hanging. Clint did not trust himself to go to a saloon. Someone would say something about Rosie and the Gunsmith knew he might very well try to kill him.

So he sat in his hotel room with a bottle of whiskey and sipped his liquor until well after midnight. He was not a man to get drunk, and his shock at the verdict given Rosie was so profound that no amount of drink could have blurred his senses.

Clint looked down into the street. He faced a decision that might change the very course of his life. Could he break the law that he had lived by so honorably all these years and free Rosie? He shook his head. Perhaps the real question is: could I allow her to hang and live with myself anymore?

The answer to the first question was yes, he could break the law. The answer to the second question was no, he could not live with himself if he allowed Rosie to swing into eternity.

Clint stood up and packed his saddlebags. He washed his face in the basin and shaved, then combed his black hair and put on a fresh shirt.

Before leaving he buckled his gunbelt and grabbed his bags. The bottle of whiskey sat on the windowsill and he left it where it was. Someone else might find some comfort in it, but he needed fresh air and a long ride across Texas.

Clint took the back stairs down to the alley and then headed for the livery stable. Twenty minutes later, he had Duke and Crimson Victory saddled and ready. He knew with certainty that he was crossing a bridge that he could not retreat back across. He would become a wanted man himself, a fugitive of the law that he had always sworn to uphold.

Clint was prepared to do that for Rosie. She had saved his life; now, he would save hers in return.

The jail was shuttered and dark inside. Clint moved to the front door and when he tried to open it, found it was locked. He walked around the jail and found a side door to the alley. It was also locked but at least he was off the main street and hidden in shadows.

"Hey in there!" he shouted in a slurred, drunken sounding voice. "Open up, Sheriff, I need a place to sleep again tonight!"

"Go away! The jail is full of women!" a sleepy voice called.

Clint took out his gun and banged the handle against the door. "Open up!" he bellowed. "I need a drink, too!"

He heard a chair scrape across the floor and Clint flattened against the wall. Suddenly, the door swung open and a block of lamplight spilled into the alley. Clint saw the man's head emerge and brought his gun butt down hard across the man's skull. The sheriff fell soundlessly and the Gunsmith slipped inside the office.

"Clint?" It was Rosie and her voice was anxious.

"That's right," he said, moving toward a keyboard and choosing the ring with the cell door keys. "And I'm taking you out of here!"

"If she goes, I go!" Lola hissed. It was a small town jail with only one cell and the women were together.

"Uh-uh."

Lola tore a long, silvery darning needle from the lining of her dress. She grabbed Rosie around the neck and shoved the needle to the base of her skull. "I've killed men with this," she swore, "and you can bet that I'll kill her before you can stop me, if you don't take me with you!"

"Don't listen to her," Rosie begged. "If she gets away this time—"

"Shut up!"

"All right," Clint breathed. "Just hold it steady and I'll let you go."

"Damn right you will!"

Clint opened the door. The needle looked to be five inches long. He stepped back as Lola pushed Rosie out into the office.

"Throw me your gun!"

Clint did as he was ordered and when Lola had it in her fist, she relaxed, then smiled. "So, this is how it ends. Get into that cell. Aren't they going to be surprised when the sheriff wakes up and comes back inside to find you instead of me behind bars."

Clint stepped in front of Rosie to shield her from a bullet. "It's not going to go that way," he said tightly. "If you use that gun on us, the whole town will come running. The saloons and streets are full. You'll never make it out alive."

Lola's hand trembled. It was checkmate. She knew that the Gunsmith wasn't running a bluff.

"All right," she said, "but I can't say it hasn't been interesting."

She turned and raced for the side door. Clint scooped up a gun and walked over to the sheriff's desk. He took the flickering kerosene lamp and smashed it across the desk. The mantle shattered as the burning liquid rivered across the desk's surface and then down onto the floor.

"Why did you do that?" Rosie asked.

Clint smiled. "I'm hoping to buy you a clean start."

They hesitated while the flames leapt up and began to climb the walls and then consume the ceiling. When a good part of the room was ablaze, the Gunsmith nodded with satisfaction.

"This ought to create a little distraction. Say goodbye to your funeral pyre, Rosie."

She took his hand and pulled him toward the door. "Please, let's hurry!"

In the side alley, Clint grabbed the unconscious sheriff and dragged him out of danger. He stopped a few seconds to hear the fire company's alarm bell begin to toll as the flames broke through the ceiling of the sheriff's office. Holstering his gun, he took

Rosie's hand and they hurried toward the livery and their waiting horses.

Suddenly, he heard gunfire.

"Stay right here in the shadows!" he yelled, racing back toward the main street.

Clint skidded to a halt as a cowboy with a smoking gun bent over Lola Perdue's body. The man was young and he swayed a little from his drinking. As several other men hurried over to investigate the shooting, Clint heard the cowboy say, "I didn't know it was that killer woman. I just saw someone try to steal my horse. I yelled for 'im to stop and when he didn't . . . I shot 'im out of the saddle."

"Good riddance!" another cowboy spat. "Let's get some buckets and help 'em form a brigade before the whole durned town burns to the ground."

The cowboy holstered his gun and shrugged. "I didn't like killin' a woman, even one that was supposed to hang tomorrow."

"Aw, it don't matter. Besides, we still got the Wade woman to hang, don't we?"

"Hell no," the cowboy said, staring at the inferno. "Like as not, she went up with the jail. This one hated the other too much to help her escape."

Clint stepped back into the alley and his stride was long and purposeful. The cowboy had stated it plainly. Clint felt his spirits lift. Maybe I really did bury Rosie Wade and give her a new life.

"What happened?" Rosie asked.

"Lola is dead."

Rosie took a step back. The Gunsmith steadied her and they hurried on to the livery. A few minutes later they were galloping out of Cut 'N Run, Texas as flames sparked high into the night. The fire was burning so hot that it would leave nothing but white cinder. The town had Lola Perdue, but Rosie was going free.

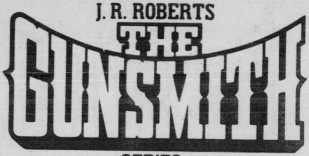

J. R. ROBERTS
THE GUNSMITH
SERIES

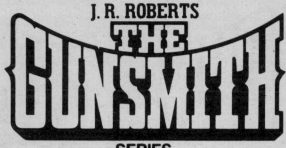

SERIES